HIS DARKNESS

HIS CONFESSION TRILOGY
BOOK 1

ANGEL RAYNE

Published by Everblood Publishing, LLC
https://everbloodpublishing.com

ISBN-978-1-945499-80-7

Cover Design by Dar at Wicked Smart Designs

Proofreader: Mackenzie @ NiceGirlNaughtyEdits.com

ALSO BY ANGEL RAYNE

Mafia Romance Reading Order

Luca and Veda

His Game

His Stakes

His Win

Enzo and Sera

His Promise

His Rejection

His Proposal

Tristan and Luna

His Darkness

His Deception

His Destiny

<u>**Stand Alone Novels**</u>

<u>**Tyler and Ailee**</u>

Be With Me

SYNOPSIS

**I'm not a villain. I'm something
much, *much* worse...**

People have called me many things over the years.
Cold. Violent. Monster. Psychopath.
Only the last one is incorrect.
I'm actually a sociopath.

But my lack of *feelings* never hurt me. In fact, it helped
me survive the brutal torture of my upbringing. Made me
one of the best mafia enforcers in the business.
So, I'm...content with my life. Or I was, at least.

Until I saw *her*.

Luna Wilde is the property of one of my boss's men.
Untouchable. Forbidden. I've been ordered to keep my
distance.
But for the first time, I don't give a single *fu*k* about my
orders.
I'm *obsessed*. Ready to stalk her to the ends of the earth
and destroy *anyone* who stands between us.
I hope she likes the dark.

Because that's where she'll stay now that she's *mine...*

"I love you as certain dark things are to be loved,

in secret, between the shadow and the soul."

-Pablo Neruda

PROLOGUE

My computer dinged with a reminder for my next appointment. A new client I've never seen before.

1 PM: John Doe

I lowered my hand—and the half of the meatball sub sandwich I was about to bite into—back onto the desk and set it on the greasy wrapper. It wasn't unusual for people who came to see me to use a fake name. Many of them were well-known in the public eye and didn't want the paparazzi to get wind of the fact they needed therapy.

I pulled up the calendar where Lydia, my assistant, scheduled my patients and jotted down the few details she'd given me into my notebook: His use of a fake name. The fact that he was a new patient. I looked for the reason he'd requested the appointment, but the space was blank.

Guess I'd have to wait and see. Honestly, I preferred it that way sometimes. Figuring out what made people tick made me hard. And I was damn good at it. That's why the A-listers came from all over to see me, and I rarely had time for new clients. So this guy must have some major pull somewhere to have worked his way onto my schedule. Or, he was paying cash up front for the appointment. And the only people who had enough money lying around to pay cash for my time were either celebrities or politicians.

I finished my sandwich and washed my hands in my private bathroom, checked my teeth and ran a brush through my hair, then looked at my watch. One o'clock on the dot. Time to meet my new mystery client.

Back at my desk, I buzzed Lydia out in the lobby. "Is the next appointment here?"

"Yes," she told me. "He's been waiting for a few minutes now." Her voice had that weird tremor that told me this particular client made her uncomfortable. I rolled my eyes for the fourth time this week. I was going to have to find a new assistant. Besides being horrifically unattractive, this one got way too star-struck for this line of work.

I opened my office door. "John?" I always liked to start on a first-name basis, even if that name was fake. It made people feel like we were already friends, making it easier for them to open up to me and spill all of their deepest, darkest secrets.

The man sitting in my waiting room stood, buttoning his suit jacket and checking his sleeves and cufflinks. I didn't recognize him, but he practically oozed power and money. One look told me his suit was made from luxurious high-end wool and was custom-tailored to fit his broad shoulders and lean frame. The close-cropped sides of his dark hair revealed a two-inch scar above his left ear. Another ran along his jawline, barely visible beneath an impeccably neat beard. I wondered how many more were hidden under his clothes.

Despite his scars, his nose was straight and there wasn't a hair out of place, which told me he valued his appearance and kept tight control over the way he looked, and probably everything else in his life. Moving with the grace of a fighter, he prowled toward me, completely owning the space he occupied. Reminding myself that I was the professional here, and he had come to see me, I smiled and extended my hand. Everything about this man made me want to put him at ease.

As he clasped my hand with a firm shake, eyes so dark they were nearly black met mine. I searched their depths for a hint of why he was here. Curiosity. Nervousness. Anger. Things I would typically see in new clients.

But his eyes were alarmingly emotionless.

A tingle of warning ran down my back as I invited him into my office. He walked past me and stopped, looking between the chairs to the right and the couch to the left near my desk. "Make yourself at home, John. Wherever you feel comfortable is fine." I shared a look with Lydia as I closed the door behind him, shutting us into my office together.

He chose the chairs. Particularly the one that would put his back to the wall. Interesting. Was he former military? Security? Or did he just have trust issues? I retrieved my notebook and pen from my desk, along with my tape recorder, and settled into the opposite chair. "How are you today?" I asked him.

"I'm fine. Thank you."

His speech was very proper, every word enunciated clearly, and I detected the hint of an accent. Italian, maybe? "Do you mind if I record our session?" When he stilled, I hurried to reassure him. "It's only for my own use inside of this office. Have you been made aware of the doctor-patient confidentiality clause?" I set the recorder on the table.

"Yes." He eyed the recorder for a moment and then shifted his eyes back to my face, but he didn't oppose having it there. Leaning back, he crossed one ankle over his knee and laced his fingers together on his lap. His shoes were just as impressive as his suit.

I pressed the button to start recording, sat back and uncapped my pen. "So, what brings you in to see me today?"

"I met a woman," he told me without hesitation.

"You met...*a woman?*" I couldn't keep the incredulousness from my voice. The last thing I'd expected from this man was to hear him say he'd come here so I could help him with his love life. I was a heavily sought-after psychiatrist with many accolades for assisting clients with severe mental health issues. No one had ever come to me for help with their schoolyard crush before.

"Yes," was all he said.

I cleared my throat and pretended to jot down some notes. "And where did you meet this girl?"

"She's a woman, not a girl. And actually, I've known her for a while now."

"And this *woman* is the only reason you came to see me?"

He thought about that for a second. "Yes."

"Why is that?"

"Because ever since I met her, it's fucked me up in the head. And I want you to tell me how to make it stop so I can go back to the way I was before."

Well, at least that gave me a place to start. Leaning forward, I gave him my full attention. Perhaps if I could put his mind at ease, this would be our one and only session. Though the money was appealing, for once Lydia was right, something about this client made me extremely uncomfortable. "What do you mean, 'the way you were before?' Why would you want to do that? People change a little when they fall in love, John. It's completely normal."

His expression never faltered as he looked down at the recorder on the table and then back at me.

A trickle of apprehension slid down my spine. I ignored it. "You have doctor-patient confidentiality, John. Nothing you say here will ever be shared outside of the two of us. Not even if they put me on the stand." I didn't actually know if that was why he hesitated, but it never hurt to give a reminder. And by the way his eyes flicked to mine, I'd say I guessed correctly.

His phone vibrated, breaking the silence, and he winced slightly as he retrieved it from his inside jacket pocket. As he did so, I noticed a thin strap that crossed his chest. Had he brought a weapon into my office? Open carry was allowed in Texas, but my rules on firearms were very clear on my website and the sign on the door to my office.

Preparing to remind him of my policy, I met his eyes as he silenced his phone and put it back in his pocket, really looking this time. Complete and utter darkness stared back at me. Cold. Calculated. Keeping eye contact, he deliberately adjusted his jacket to cover the holster strap, making it perfectly clear he couldn't care less about my rules and policies. A deduction confirmed by his next answer.

"I'm not normal. And I'm not in love. I locked her in a fucking cage."

His answer jolted my attention from the possible weapon he was carrying, and my eyes flew back to his face. No expression whatsoever to reveal how he felt about what he'd done.

I held up one hand, palm out. "Before you say more, I need to make sure you're clear on the confidentiality agreement. It's no longer applicable if I believe you're a danger to yourself or someone else."

He stared at me with those cold, dead eyes. "I would never hurt her. That's the whole fucking problem."

"But you *want* to hurt her?" I should probably put an end to this right fucking now. But I couldn't help but be intrigued. Despite the anger in his tone, his expression continued to show no emotion whatsoever. It was the most fascinating thing I'd ever seen. Also, if I could find out where he was hiding this woman, I could sell the information to a crooked cop I knew and give him the opportunity to play hero. It was always good to be owed favors.

"No. I locked her up to keep *him* from hurting her."

"Okay. Okay." I took a deep breath and sat back in my chair. He was showing some concern. At least that gave me something to work with. "Does she have a name?"

His eyes narrowed. "Jane."

Of course. "How long have you kept Jane locked up?"

"A few weeks."

"And you haven't hurt her?"

"No. I told you, I can't."

"Are you planning to let her out?"

He thought about it for a second, then shook his head. "No. She's safer in there."

"So, what do you want from me?"

Visibly agitated now, he got to his feet and ran a hand through his hair as he began to pace. "I want you to fix me. Undo whatever the fuck she did to make me feel all of this shit, like I need to protect her. To make me *feel* at all."

The man was clearly unstable. As he turned back to face me, something new caught my eye—a bright red stain seeping through his white shirt, just above the waistband of his pants.

I came half out of my chair before I caught myself. "You're bleeding!"

He didn't stop his pacing or even bother to look down at his shirt. "Yes."

"Why are you bleeding?"

"Because she shot me," he said distractedly.

I stood up, my notepad falling to the floor. "What are you doing here? Why the hell didn't you go to the hospital?"

He tilted his head, looking at me with a furrowed brow. But again, it was his eyes that really scared me. Like looking into a black hole. "I didn't want to be late for my appointment."

He didn't want to... "You need to go to the hospital." I wanted this man out of my office, and this was the perfect excuse. I walked to my desk and pressed the intercom. "Lydia, call an ambulance for Mr..."

The slide of a bullet being loaded into the chamber made me freeze. I looked over to find the barrel of a pistol pointed directly at my face. "No ambulance."

My entire body went cold, and I froze. Holding up my free hand, I swallowed hard. "Lydia, cancel the ambulance."

"Are you sure?" she asked on the speakerphone. "Are you okay?"

"Everything's fine," I lied. "Why don't you go ahead and take your lunch now?" I lifted my finger off the button and lowered my hand.

"Can you fix me or not?" he asked.

I paused, a lie on the tip of my tongue. But even with a gun pointed at me, somehow, I didn't think I'd be able to get away with lying to this man. "I'm sorry, but other than prescribing you something akin to a tranquilizer, there isn't anything I can do to keep you from caring about someone. It just...happens sometimes. Whether we want it to or not."

A muscle in his jaw twitched.

"Look," I told him, discreetly wiping the sweat from my palms as I tried to de-escalate the situation. "How about you lower that weapon and we can talk about this some more. I can help you work through these feelings you're having so they don't seem so overwhelming."

"I don't think you understand." The gun remained pointed at my face. "If you can't fix me, I'll lose everything."

I spread my hands wide. "What you're asking just isn't possible. I can't just medicate your feelings away, but if you'll just let me..."

"No," he told me. "We're done here." Reaching into his jacket pocket, he pulled out a silencer. Calmly and meticulously, like he'd done it a thousand times, he attached it to the end of the barrel. When his cold, dead eyes returned to my face, they stared through me like I was already nothing more than a memory.

The realization that these were the last minutes of my life punched me in the gut, and the sour smell of my urine burned my nose as warm piss soaked my underwear and trickled down my leg.

I couldn't keep the panic from my voice. "You don't have to do this. I can help you."

"No, you can't."

"I can," I insisted.

"Nothing personal, Doc. But this was a mistake. Thank you for patronizing me, but this appointment is over."

My last emotion wasn't fear. It was a feeling of surprise. I always imagined silencers to be...well...silent. But they weren't. Not completely...

CHAPTER 1

Tristan

Two Months Earlier

I'm not a man.

Not really.

Not like other men.

What I am is a human bullet shield for my boss, Luca. And occasionally for Enzo, Luca's other personal soldier, if the need arises. A job I was groomed for by Luca's father ever since I was a young child. A job I'm more than happy to show up for every day.

Maybe happy isn't the right word. Indifferent might be more accurate. Not about Luca himself. He and Enzo are probably the closest thing to friends I'd ever have. But it's not like I give a shit about what happens to me. Only what happens to them. However, I don't know if it's because I genuinely care, or because I've been trained to do so.

And that bothers me a little sometimes.

However, today...today, as I watched Enzo and Serafina exchange vows, it was the first time I could remember feeling...something. Anything. And it had nothing at all to do with my friend and his new wife, but rather, one of their guests.

As I watched the dark-haired beauty walk into Luca's home on Gino's arm in a red dress that flirted with her curves and only teased at what was underneath, that *thing* stirred deep within my chest. That same thing I'd noticed when I first saw her sitting there in the setting sun during the wedding ceremony. It was primitive and possessive and utterly unfamiliar to me, and it made me want to sink my knife into Gino's fat gut and gift her with a necklace of his intestines.

I almost didn't recognize what it was at first. Emotions of any kind weren't something I was used to experiencing. And the tightening in my chest surprised me so much that I stopped and took a deep breath, taking stock of my body, wondering if an old injury was acting up.

But no. It wasn't anything physical.

How strange.

"Who is that woman?" I asked Luca when he and Veda stopped alongside me. "The one with Gino."

He followed my gaze to the woman I couldn't stop staring at. "I heard she was payment for a gambling debt that was owed to him," he told me. Veda looked at the woman with new interest, and I could tell she was disturbed by his answer. That didn't surprise me. She wasn't from our world, and she was still soft.

However, these types of things happened all the time. It never bothered me before. It wasn't my business. So why was it, with this woman, I suddenly wanted to *make* it my business?

"Tris? What is it?"

Tearing my eyes away from the woman's smooth, bare legs—that I could now clearly see across the room as the crowd parted, along with the four-inch black heels she wore with her red dress—I turned back to Luca. "I just feel like I know her from somewhere." Not exactly the truth, but not quite a lie, and it was a reason Luca would readily accept.

From the corner of my eye, I saw him glance her way again before his attention came back to me. "She does look familiar." He glanced at her again and frowned. Then shook his head slightly. "It doesn't matter. I would forget about her if I were you," Luca warned. "She's Gino's property now. And you know how he gets. I don't want to rock the boat with him right now."

As I watched Gino slide his hand over her ass and squeeze it, my skin crawled, and I nodded in agreement. I didn't want to rock the boat either.

I wanted to fucking sink it.

Luca took that opportunity to change the subject. "But speaking of Gino, I need to discuss a few things with him about his son, Salvatore. If he can't get that boy under control, he's going to start a fucking war."

"Still going after the Irish?" Salvatore had shot one of them in a club not too long ago. Luckily, Salvatore's brother, Gildo, had been there and knocked the gun away so the bullet only grazed the other man. The club owner, however, was the victim's older brother and the leader of their gang, and Gino had had to dish out a lot of money and a few favors to calm him down. Last I'd heard, the matter had been settled.

"Just one Irishman in particular, it appears. And I'm about to find out why." He turned to Veda, and I watched as his eyes devoured her face like he wanted to memorize every feature. I didn't understand their connection, yet I couldn't tear my eyes away. Taking both of her hands in his, he lifted them to his mouth and kissed her knuckles. "Will you be okay until I get back, amore?"

She smiled at him. "I'll be fine. I'm gonna go congratulate the bride and groom." She raised her face to his and gave him a lingering kiss, then smiled at me in the timid way she always did and walked away. I made her uncomfortable, but it didn't bother me. Most people gave off that vibe when I was around them. However, there was no need for her to feel that way. I would never do anything to harm her, no matter the circumstances, because I knew if I did, Luca wouldn't like it. Perhaps I should talk to her sometime and explain this to her. It might help her to relax around me. This was her home now, after all. And I was a permanent fixture in it, as was Enzo.

I followed Luca to the bar where Gino was handing the dark-haired woman a drink in a martini glass. She had removed the cream-colored fur from her shoulders and tucked it beneath one arm, showing off the short sleeves of her dress and her upper arms. There were two freckles on her left bicep just above her elbow, one slightly larger than the other, but otherwise, her skin was unmarred as far as I could see. Her face and arms were unmarked by piercings or tattoos, except for one hole in each of her ears, which told me she didn't blow her money on frivolous things. She glanced over at me when we approached, then nervously lowered her eyes so her dark eyelashes hid her thoughts from me and took a sip of her drink. Her long hair, so dark it was nearly black, was pulled back on one side and fell in soft waves over her shoulders and down her back. My hands fisted at my sides, imagining those thick, silky strands intertwined with my fingers. And I suddenly wished we were alone so I could see what it looked like against the pale skin of her breasts.

My cock swelled at the thought.

Frowning at my body's reaction, I studied her, wondering why I was fantasizing about this girl. Sex, for me, was used solely as a release of tension. Something I only sought out occasionally and did alone.

"Luca!" Gino interrupted my thoughts as he grasped Luca's hand and leaned in with pursed lips to press them upon both of his cheeks in the old way of greeting. Tension tightened my shoulders as I watched him. Still, it amused me to see how big of a kiss-ass he'd become since Luca had risen from underboss to boss in the family.

"Gino," Luca responded, not quite as warmly. "May I have a quick moment of your time, *per favore?*"

"Eh, can't it wait?" Gino waved his wineglass in a wide arc, taking in the room of people laughing and drinking around them. I watched as it sloshed dangerously close to the edge of the glass and then onto the expensive floors of Luca's lake house. "This is a celebration! Not a time for business."

Without taking his eyes from Gino, Luca gestured at one of the servers hired for the event and pointed to the spilled wine. "I'm afraid it really can't wait," he told him, pulling him aside so the server could clean up the mess he'd made.

The grin on Gino's face faltered for a moment before it came back in full force. He glanced at the woman beside him, then back at Luca. "Are you certain it can't wait until tomorrow, at least? It's Luna's first night out, and I hate to leave her all by herself."

Luna.

Her name locked into my memory.

"I'm sorry, but I'm afraid it can't," Luca insisted.

Gino studied him for a moment, then, with a great sigh, set his glass down on the bar. "Your father would never be so uncouth as to discuss business during a wedding."

"My father is dead," was Luca's simple reply. "God rest his soul."

Gino eyed Luca. "*Sì*, I know."

It was no secret that some of the Cosa Nostra believed Luigi had been prematurely removed from his seat as head of this family, and that it had been done under Luca's orders, which wasn't entirely true. However, Gino was the only one who had the balls to say it, more or less, to Luca's face.

Luca ignored the jibe. "It's important, *mio amico*," My friend. "And it will only take a few minutes. When we return to the party, I'll buy you a drink."

"Ah, but you already have." Gino lifted his wineglass, "Since it's an open bar. But how about a dance with your *bella donna*, eh?"

Gino's eyes wandered over to where Veda stood, laughing with the new bride, and I idly wondered if he was aware of how very near to death he was at this very moment.

"I'm afraid Veda's dance card is full for tonight," Luca told him evenly. Even so, something about his tone had Gino glancing at his hard blue eyes before quickly looking away and bowing his head.

"Of course. My loss," he said with a smile as he tried to smooth things over again. "Besides, I have this one to dance with." He cocked his head toward his date. "Stay here," he ordered Luna, setting his empty glass on the bar. "I'll be back in a few minutes." Then his eyes wandered over to me, and he lifted a hand to clap me on the shoulder. "Tristan here will keep you company until then, yes?"

I took an immediate step back out of his reach, my spine stiffening for a brief instant before I forced myself to relax, then glanced over at Luca, who gave me a slight nod. "It would be my honor," I told Gino.

He gave Luna a look I couldn't quite decipher. "Make sure she doesn't leave the party early," he told me without taking his eyes from her. "I promised her a good time tonight, and I intend to deliver on that promise."

The words were said lightly, but the meaning behind them was clear. She was here because he wanted her here, and she would stay until he decided they would leave. My teeth began to ache, and I unclenched my jaw and relaxed my hands, which had started to form into fists.

From the corner of my eye, I saw her take a long drink, and something twisted in my gut. "She'll be here when you return."

Luca glanced between me and Luna. I sensed his hesitation to leave me alone with her, even though he'd given his permission. Clearing his throat to get my attention, he gave me a warning look and led the old capo toward the hallway leading to his office.

Once they were gone, I gave in to my curiosity and studied the woman beside me. What was it about her that held my attention hostage?

She was stunning, with her cobalt blue eyes, dark hair, and full lips, but I was around beautiful women all the time at Luca's clubs. And they were usually naked, or nearly so. And yet, they'd never earned more than a moment of my appreciation.

But this one—Luna—she was...captivating. It made me feel uneasy.

I took a step closer and caught a whiff of an old-fashioned perfume that seemed vaguely familiar. She glanced at me from the corner of her eye and sipped her drink. Was I making her nervous? I should probably give her some space and stop staring like a goddamn creep, but I couldn't seem to drag my attention away.

After what seemed to be an eternity, she spoke to me. "So, Tristan, huh?"

The sultry notes of her voice flowed over me like warm water, relaxing my muscles and increasing the flow of blood through my veins as it rushed to my cock. I was getting hard again just hearing the sound of my name on her lips. Fascinating. "Yes."

"I'm Luna."

"I know."

She nodded and gave me an uncomfortable smile before looking away again to watch the people milling about the great room.

"What's your last name?" I asked her.

"Wilde. With an 'e.'"

I tried to remember if I knew that name, but it wouldn't come to me.

"And yours?"

"De Stefano," I said distractedly.

"Tristan De Stefano," she repeated. "That's a nice name."

"Thank you."

With a glance and a slight lift of the corners of her lips that wasn't quite a smile, she turned her face toward the sound of the band that was drifting in through the open patio doors. Some of the guests began to drift back outside to listen to them.

I watched as Luna's chest rose and fell with a deep breath. Then she set down her drink and turned to me. "So, do you wanna dance?"

"No," I told her.

She blinked at my brusque answer, something vulnerable flashing in her eyes right before she ducked her head. But when she lifted her chin again, it was gone, replaced by calm confidence she'd pulled over herself like a shield.

There was more to this woman than a gorgeous face and body. Much more.

My eyes traveled over her face, and then followed the elegant line of her neck down to her shoulders and arms and the swell of her breasts, wondering what she looked like beneath the silky material of her dress. Perfect. I'd bet she was perfect. But it wasn't just her physical looks that drew me to her. No. There was something else. A honed strength that shone from her eyes and appeared in the set of her shoulders.

"Um...okay." Her forehead creased in confusion. "You don't know how?"

My eyes found hers. "I know how. I don't want to." Dancing required touching. I wasn't good with touching unless it was absolutely necessary.

"Oh."

A slight red flush blossomed on the pale skin at the neckline of her dress. I watched, fascinated, as it spread up her throat to her cheeks like a fog creeping across an open field.

She cleared her throat and picked up her drink again. "Guess we'll just stand here awkwardly until my owner gets back then."

I frowned, disliking her choice of words. "Your owner?"

"Yeah. That's what he is," she told me. Then she shrugged one shoulder. "But I did it to myself, so I can't even be mad about it. And that's what really irritates me the most."

"What did you do?"

"I lost," she said with a self-deprecating smile. "That's what I did. I lost the bet."

So what Luca had heard was true.

"But I didn't lose everything. Just myself." She gave me another strange smile that didn't reach her eyes. "I'm kinda used to that."

I wanted to ask what she meant, but we were out of time to talk. Luca and Gino were returning. I tried to read Luca's expression as they rejoined us, but he was locked down tight. That couldn't be good. Gino, on the other hand, was all smiles as he signaled to the bartender for a refill. I felt, more than saw, Luna's entire body stiffen at the return of Gino, and her words echoed around in my head.

I narrowed my eyes as he wrapped an arm around her waist and dropped a kiss on her shoulder, images of him sliding her dress down and pressing his wet lips to her bare skin making my skin hot and prickly.

"Tristan."

It took me a moment to realize Luca was trying to get my attention. "Hmm?"

He stepped closer, blocking my view of Gino. "I mean it," he said, so low I could barely hear him. "Leave her alone."

I wondered idly if Gino was treating her well. By the stiff set of her spine and shoulders, I would guess the answer to that question would be no. It made my skin itch to think of his hands on her, and I frowned...

"Tristan."

Luca's tone had changed. "Yes?"

"I need you to relieve Paulie outside. Watch the gate. All of the guests are here. No one else should be coming in."

I nodded once to indicate I understood, then strode purposefully across the room to the front door, checking my weapon discreetly as I went. I never thought to question the order. And I didn't look back at the woman with Gino again. But I didn't need to. Her image was seared into my brain.

Besides, I would see her again soon. Very soon.

CHAPTER 2

Tristan

It wasn't easy to get onto Gino's property, but I managed, and I only had to take out one of his guards to do it. Later...much later...it would occur to me that Luca wouldn't be happy about that. But in the moment, the only thing on my mind was seeing *her* again.

Luna.

She'd taken up a permanent residence in my head since I'd left the wedding reception earlier that evening to watch the front gate, per Luca's order. And even though I knew Gino would want to show off his winnings every chance he could, and I'd have plenty of opportunities to see her again, it wasn't good enough. I couldn't wait. Something drew me to this woman. Something that tugged at my ribcage deep within my chest. And I found myself standing outside of Gino's house mere hours after we'd met, searching for a glimpse of her like some kind of fucked up stalker.

The old house where Gino resided was a sprawling one-story with a high wall surrounding it that took up nearly half of the two-acre lot and gave the occupants a false sense of security. Ideally, Gino should have twice as many guards as he did. More men on the wall, and at least four more patrolling the property. And where were his cameras? It had been ridiculously easy for me to scale the wall in a darkened corner of the yard and stay in the shadows as I snuck up to his home.

As ornery as Gino was, it was a miracle the man was still alive, being so exposed. He might as well be standing in the middle of a field, an open target to his enemies. As was anyone else in this house. There was no way in hell I would've been able to sneak onto Luca's estate, and I was tempted to knock on Gino's front door and inform him of how easy it was for me to get past his guards. But for now, this suited my purposes. Perhaps after, I'd offer to help Gino improve his security.

After what, I didn't know. Just...after.

Gino's home also had an obscene number of windows, no drapes or blinds hiding what went on behind closed doors, and it took me under a minute to locate her in a room on the left side of the house.

The next thought that came to my mind was that he was putting *her* in danger by being so lax with his security.

What if it wasn't me sneaking onto his property but someone who wanted to fuck Gino up and didn't give a shit who they went through to do it? A flash of anger scorched through me, so icy cold it burned within my veins, and my hand hovered over the pistol strapped to my side.

But then I took a breath and released it on a hard exhale, my breath misting in the damp night air as I walked closer, remembering why I was here. And that reason had nothing to do with Gino, and everything to do with the woman he'd had on his arm today.

Once again, the intensity of my anger took me by surprise and gave me pause. Besides, what was I going to do? Shoot Gino myself for being too cocky? He was Italian. Many of the old-school *mafiosi* were the same. Of course, the majority of them were also dead now. However, if I killed him here, tonight, Luca would know it was me, and he would have to act accordingly as the boss of *La Cosa Nostra*, the Italian mafia here in Austin. And if I was taken out of the picture, no one would be here to protect her.

I didn't like that thought.

A sudden movement in the window directly in front of me caught my attention.

The large windowpane rattled as Luna slammed against it so hard I heard her cry out as she collided, her hands up as though she'd tried to stop herself from falling through.

The light behind her was so bright it created a halo around her body and made her red dress appear black. Her head was turned, the side of her face pressed against the glass.

Staying within the shadows, I moved closer. Her eyes were squeezed closed. Her pretty mouth twisted in a grimace of pain.

Her silhouette changed as her dress was lifted and bunched around her waist. Her hips jerked back, and then she hit the glass again. Someone stood behind her, his hand slamming into the pane above her head.

Gino.

And he was tearing off her panties.

Gino's hand left the glass, dropping to her head and tangling in her long, dark hair, jerking her head back. My muscles tensed, and a red haze colored my vision as the woman who hadn't left my mind since I'd first seen her earlier that evening stumbled back awkwardly in her heels, arms flailing. With one hand gripping her hair and the other pressed between her shoulder blades, Gino led her over to the bed and bent her over the end with her ass in the air.

Stiff and still, she waited as Gino struggled one-handed with the opening to his brown slacks. I took a step forward. Then stopped. There was a roaring in my ears. Why didn't she try to get up? Was this a game they played? Did she enjoy it rough?

Unsettled, I paced back and forth within the shadow of the oak tree, my fists clenched and my eyes never leaving the scene inside. Of course, he would fuck her. He'd won her, after all. As she said earlier, she belonged to him now. That's how it was in our world. So why did seeing it with my own eyes affect me so much?

Gino palmed her bare ass, and I couldn't help but sneak closer, wondering what her skin would feel like beneath my own hands. What she would taste like between her plump thighs. I couldn't even imagine. I'd never been with a woman, or anyone, for that matter. The only intimacy I'd ever known was the feel of a leather strap tearing into my skin. Or the embrace of water as it filled every orifice until there was no more air. A more peaceful way to die, honestly, once you stopped fighting it. And one that I would prefer if I had the chance to choose.

But I'd never felt skin on skin. Not like this. Not since I was a child. The few times someone touched me when I wasn't expecting it, the feeling was so alien and unpleasant I'd pull away immediately. On really bad days, I'd freeze in terror for a split second, my body caught in a fight or flight response before my mind caught up with what was happening.

So, yeah, uninitiated touching wasn't something I accepted easily.

Watching Gino touch her so casually, though...I was both extremely uncomfortable and unequivocally jealous. I resumed pacing, strangely enthralled by the scene playing out before me. I didn't even think to try to stop him. Instead, I wiped the sweat from my upper lip with the back of my hand and watched, fascinated, as I imagined it was me standing behind her. Me touching her. Living vicariously through another man as he did the things I wished with every cell of my being that I could do.

Or at least he tried.

By the time he finally got his dick free, Luna had apparently decided she wasn't in the mood after all. Twisting around, she slid away, her dress ripping as Gino tried to pin her to the bed. She bolted, running toward the door in one shoe. With a roar of rage, he charged across the room, catching her as she reached for the doorknob and throwing her back toward the bed.

She stumbled and fell across it, partially out of my view, her desperate cry cut off with a gasp as Gino's full weight landed on top of her. I now knew for certain that this was no game. I took a step forward. Stopped.

A cold sweat broke out across my skin. Closing my eyes, I tried to block out the scene unfolding in front of me. But it was impossible when I could hear Luna's cries and Gino's curses through the thin panes of glass.

I turned around and left the same way I'd come in. I'd seen and heard enough. There was nothing I could do for her right now. If I barged into the room, his guards within the house—if there were any—would be on me in seconds. And even if I was lucky enough not to get shot, Luca would find out I'd directly disobeyed his orders and come here.

No, I just needed to get home.

By the time I reached the car, pain was squeezing my rib cage and my throat was closing up. The SUV was unlocked, and as soon as I reached it I ripped open the driver's side door and threw myself inside.

Breathe.

Just fucking breathe.

My foot on the brake, I tried to push the start button, but as the fragmented memories of my past washed over me, my hands shook so fucking much my finger kept jabbing the dash all around it instead. "Come on. Come on," I murmured. Finally, I hit it and heard the engine turn over. I slammed my foot on the gas pedal and got the hell out of there as fast as I could. I couldn't be found. Not now. I needed to get home before I was lost to the darkness.

About halfway back to Luca's property, I realized the car was beeping at me and saw the seatbelt light flashing. Reaching over my shoulder, I pulled the belt across my body but had no luck securing it, so I just let it go.

I just needed to fucking get home.

Demons from the past preyed on my emotions, swooping down at me within the small space of the vehicle with bared fangs and sharp claws. Snapping at my mind.

I thought about pulling over and calling Enzo. He would come and get me. Make sure I got home and put me where I was safe. He never asked any questions. But he had a new wife. And we weren't young kids anymore. I could get myself there. I just had. To. Keep. Going.

Gritting my teeth against the screams rising inside of me, I kept driving.

By the time I made it to Luca's, I could no longer contain them, and I raged at things and people no one could see but me. I tore down the long drive, swerving to the left when I reached the turnoff. When I saw the small house I lived in illuminated by the headlights, I started to tremble violently.

Almost there.

I don't remember parking the SUV or getting out of it. I only realized where I was when my shaking hands unlocked the door to the back bedroom and I saw the iron bars of the cell inside. Stumbling across the room, I threw myself into the cage and pulled the door shut with a loud clang. Then I locked myself inside and gripped the key so tight in my fist it cut into the skin of my palm.

Stumbling backward, I hit the wall as sweat stung my eyes. I struggled to get enough air as the phantom pain of a whip tearing into my back set my skin on fire and angry voices ricocheted through my aching head. My legs gave out, and I sank to the floor, fighting for every breath.

Safe.

I was safe.

No one could get to me in here.

I reached blindly for the blanket beside me and wrapped it around my head and shoulders, my muscles twitching with remembered pain and shame, then laid down on the hard floor, waiting for my heart to slow and the shaking to stop. It *would* stop. Eventually.

I just had to hang on. Nothing could touch me in here. The voices berating me weren't real. The fists hitting me weren't really there. I wouldn't wake up bruised and bloody.

He wouldn't come for me.

I was safe in my cell.

CHAPTER 3

Luna

Twelve Years Ago

"I don't like this place, Luni."

I stopped unpacking his suitcase and looked over at my little brother, Logan. He was only ten years old and already almost as tall as I was at fourteen. "It'll be okay, Logi." I grinned when he scowled at me for making fun of the nickname he'd used for me ever since he started talking. Back when our mom was still alive.

He'd always been a scowly kid, though. Grumbly by nature. But his grouchiness with me never lasted long, and this instance proved no different from any other.

Looking around the large bedroom he'd been given at the opposite end of the hall from mine, his eyes filled with tears. "I want to be in the same room as you."

"Hey." I dropped the clothes I was holding and crossed the floor to pull him into a hug. "It'll be okay. We're still together, and that's what matters. Plus, I'm right down the hall." This was our third foster home since our mom was killed almost five years ago. The people who took us in weren't always the best kind of people, but we could deal with just about anything if it meant the system didn't split us up. I kept one arm around his skinny shoulders and squeezed. "Besides, you're getting way too big to share my girly room. You're gonna need your own space. What if you meet a girl you like and want to invite her over?"

He immediately made a face. "Eww. No. You're the only girl I like, Luni."

I took a step back and brushed his soft, dark hair off his forehead with my free hand. "We're gonna be okay here. You'll see. Mr. And Mrs. Phillips seem like decent people."

Logan wasn't convinced. And honestly, I wasn't either. Mr. Phillips wasn't a big man, only about five foot eight, with a paunchy gut he covered with dress shirts and fancy ties, but I could immediately tell he was the one in charge of this household. That wasn't what had me on guard, though. The weirdest thing was how his smile never reached his eyes when he talked to us. And he was the only one who ever did the talking, while his much larger wife stood behind him and said nothing, if she was even in the room at all.

With a resigned sigh, Logan walked over to his suitcase and started helping me unpack his things. After a moment, I followed him.

It would be okay. Everything would be okay.

I would make sure of it.

Eleven Years Ago

"So, can I go?"

Mr. Phillips chewed the peas he'd just shoveled into his mouth and looked down the table to where my now eleven-year-old brother was bouncing in his seat beside me, his fork paused halfway to his mouth in his excitement. Then Mr. Phillips' eyes shifted over to me. "Well, I don't know, buddy. What do you think, Luna? Can we let him go to summer camp and live without him for a week? It's not cheap, but I think we can swing the cost if you think he should go."

My stomach tightened, threatening to evacuate the meatloaf and potatoes I'd just eaten. This was the game we played, and I'd learned the rules within the first few months of living here. If Logan or I needed anything, Mr. Phillips was happy to get it for us—for a price. And that price was paid by me.

Always by me.

It started out simple. Logan needed a new backpack for school? No problem. As long as I did a few extra chores to "pay" for it under Mr. Phillips' watchful eye. My brother wanted a little spending money to grab a snack during school? Absolutely. As long as I stayed up and watched television on the couch with our foster dad, even though there was plenty of other furniture to sit on. Logan outgrew his clothes and needed new ones? Sure. Not a problem, he'd tell me with that half-faced smile. Why don't you get some, too? But I'll come with you, and I want you to try everything on for me. And why don't you try on these little shorts and this tiny bathing suit? Just for fun...

It wasn't the most comfortable life for me. Mr. Phillips was a perv who liked young girls. And every day when I got out of the shower, I'd stare at my growing boobs and widening hips and the hair that now grew where I'd never had any before, and my eyes would fill with tears. While most girls my age were wearing clothes that showed off every curve they legally could, I hid behind too-tight bras, baggy shirts, and loose pants. I never wore a pretty skirt because I wasn't stupid. Skirts were easy access to private areas of my body, and I always tried my best not to tempt him.

But otherwise, this foster home wasn't that bad. Mrs. Phillips fed us well, kept the house clean, and seemed to genuinely enjoy having us here, even if she didn't talk to us all that much. Behind her sad smile and concerned eyes, I could see she knew what was going on with me and her husband, but I also knew that she'd never stand up to him.

I was on my own.

I didn't resent her for this. Like us, she was entirely dependent on the man. And honestly, I think she was a little afraid of him. I wasn't sure why. I'd never seen him lift a hand to her. But that didn't mean there wasn't something going on behind closed doors that I didn't know about. She was only trying to survive. Just like us.

Then there were the nights when Mr. Phillips didn't come home at all. Those nights were happy and carefree for Logan and me as we ate dinner with Mrs. Phillips and told her about our days. She'd make the best dinners on those nights, things she never made for her husband, like fancy chicken cutlets with lemon or lasagna and garlic bread. And later we'd pick a movie to watch and she'd make popcorn and let us have soda and we'd all sit around and throw popcorn at the television and complain loudly about how stupid the ending was or how gross the kissing was. That last part was for Logan's sake. He wouldn't be interested in kissing anyone for a few years yet.

As for me, I'd never kissed anyone yet, either. I'd never even been on a date. But I would. Someday. When my brother was grown, and we were in our own place. And I didn't have to worry about leaving him alone in a house with people who weren't our real parents. Until that time, I'd be sticking close to him.

It was a few months before my sixteenth birthday when I found out where Mr. Phillips was going those nights he didn't come home. Logan had been gone for two nights, and so far, he hadn't come up with a way for me to "pay" for my brother's summer camp. And I found out why.

He had a new game to teach me.

I was finishing up the dishes on Tuesday night after Mrs. Phillips said she had a migraine and went to bed early when he wandered into the kitchen. "Hey, Luna. Are you about done?"

My heart jumped into my throat at the sound of his voice. "Um. Just about." I didn't ask him why he wanted to know. I never asked questions that would encourage him to keep conversing with me.

"I had an idea that I thought might be fun."

Finishing up the last pieces of silverware, I rinsed them off and put them in the dishwasher without responding. I could feel his eyes on my ass when I bent too close to the dishwasher door, even wearing baggy jean shorts that came practically to my knees and an oversized T-shirt like a skater. I'd never been on a skateboard in my life, but I'd convinced him it was the "style" in school.

"I'm sure you know that summer camp is pretty damn expensive," he told me. "And at first, I was thinking you could make it up to me by helping around the yard and such like you usually do. But then I realized you'd be pulling weeds forever if I did that. So, I thought we could play some cards instead. I need the practice for my poker nights. And if you win, you won't have to earn back the privilege of Logan getting to go to camp. What do you think?"

I turned around slowly, the sponge I'd been using to wipe up the counter still in my hand. "I don't know how to play poker."

"I'll teach you."

Yeah, right. He'd probably cheat. And there's no way I would know. He was cornering me into something I knew instinctively would change my life living here. I didn't know how I knew this. I just did. I could feel it in the tense way he held his shoulders and how he kept peeking toward the master bedroom, where his wife was probably lying in bed with a cold washcloth over her eyes like she always did when she claimed she had a migraine. "I really don't mind doing yard work," I told him. "And maybe I could help Mrs. Phillips with more stuff around the house."

"Aww, come on now. What fun is that? Let me teach you how to play poker. You'll be glad I did someday."

I tried again. "I have homework. And I have no money." Something he damn well knew.

"You don't need any money for this."

I stared at him for a long time, watching his hands as he tossed the deck of cards he held back and forth. Though he'd removed his shoes and jacket, he still wore the tan slacks and white button-down shirt he'd worn to work that morning. There was a bulge in the front of his pants I hadn't noticed earlier. I tore my eyes away. "And what if I lose?" I whispered.

A slow smile spread across his face, reaching all the way up to his eyes. It creeped me the hell out."Well, Luna, if you lose, then you'll have to pay me by doing whatever we bet."

I felt water dripping on my bare foot and looked down to see my hand squeezing the forgotten sponge. Quickly, I turned around and put it on the back of the sink, then grabbed the dish towel and bent down to wipe up the floor. "I can get a job," I told him. "Pay you back that way."

"No, Luna, you can't. Not until you're sixteen. And even then, you don't have a car, and there's no public transportation out here. How would you get to work?"

"I'd find a ride. Or call an Uber."

"Now you're just being silly. Why would you want to put anyone out like that? And you need money for an Uber. Even if you find someone to hire you, you won't get paid for at least a week or maybe two. How would you get back and forth?"

The design of the tiles around my feet blurred as tears filled my eyes. I stood up before he could see them and hung the towel back where it was.

"Come on, girl. You're making too big of a fuss out of this. We're just gonna play a little cards. It's early. You'll have plenty of time to do homework." Walking over to the four-seat kitchen table, he moved the bowl of fruit from the center and set it on the counter behind him.

Desperately, I tried to think of another way out of this. The way Mr. Phillips kept looking at me made my skin crawl. But tonight, he'd been touchier than usual— brushing up against me when he passed me on his way to the table and pulling my chair closer to his while we ate. But Logan had gone to summer camp, and I needed to pay for it. Without a job, I was at my foster father's mercy, or he wouldn't allow Logan to do anything like this again. Or worse.

I wracked my brain, but I couldn't think of anything to say that would distract him. Wiping my eyes, I glanced toward the bedroom where Mrs. Phillips was resting, and then back at the sink. I couldn't count on any help from her. Even if I screamed for help, she'd probably just stuff her head under a pillow, and tomorrow, she'd be in here making breakfast with her big smile and her sad eyes, pretending nothing had happened.

He sat down, pulled the cards out of the box, and started shuffling them. "It sure would be a shame if it got to be too much for us to have you both here. When they asked us if we'd take you and your brother, the state made it clear they couldn't find anyone else who would take in two kids. Most people are only willing to take one. And, ya know, I can't blame them. It's a lot to open your home to strangers, kids or not." He kept shuffling, but his eyes lifted to meet mine. "I mean, you never know who you're bringing into your home. You two could've been a couple of drug addicts, for all we knew. Could've robbed us blind. And that's not what we wanted. We wanted a couple of nice kids who would give my wife some company and make our lives a little easier. So, are you gonna make my life easier, Luna?"

I wanted to believe he was lying. But what if he wasn't? What if no one else would take us? We were in a nice neighborhood here. We didn't get slapped around. We were fed and taken care of. And there were no bugs in our beds. Logan was doing great in school and had even made some friends. My grades were good, too. I liked my teachers. And the other kids were actually pretty decent for high school kids, even if I hadn't made any good friends. But that was kind of my own fault. I didn't nurture any relationships because I didn't want people to start asking me to hang out or wanting to come over.

It could be so much worse for us.

I can handle this, I told myself. I could. I could handle Mr. Phillips for a few years until I turned eighteen and could petition the courts for custody of Logan. I could do it for Logan. As long as no one touched him, I could do it.

To make sure my little brother got the best chance he could at life.

Wiping the palms of my hands on the front of my shorts, I walked slowly over to the table and pulled out the chair across from him. "Okay."

He smiled at me again. "This is gonna be fun. You'll see." He started dealing the cards. "How about we start easy with some five-card draw."

"What are the bets?" I asked him. Icy fingers slid down my spine when he just looked at me and smiled.

"We'll get to that. Let me deal these cards." He gave us both five cards, face down on the table. "Okay. Now look at your hand."

I picked up the cards and looked at them. I had a pair of twos, a queen, a five, and an eight.

"The rules are whoever has the best hand wins. And you can trade in up to three of your cards for new ones if you don't like what you're holding."

I had no idea what I was holding. I looked across the table at Mr. Phillips, trying to tell what he had by his expression, but I couldn't read him. "What's a winning hand?"

"A winning hand can be anything from a royal flush to a couple of pairs. It depends on what the other players have."

I looked down at my hand again. I had no idea what a royal flush was, but I did have a pair of twos. "Does it matter what the pair is?" I asked. I was giving away my hand, but I thought this was important to know.

"Nope." Mr. Phillips finished rearranging the cards in his hand. "Okay, now we bet."

I hesitated. "But I haven't traded any of my cards yet."

"You'll do that after we bet," he told me.

"But you just traded some of your cards."

"I forgot to take the jokers out."

He was lying. But since I had no clue what the rules were, I couldn't prove it, and all I could do for now was take his word for it.

"Ya know, I've been thinking. Instead of you betting your brother's entire week of summer camp in one game, how about you bet a day at a time." Turning in his chair, he opened the drawer beneath the counter nearest him and pulled out a pad of paper and a pen. "We'll keep track on here," he said.

Knowing I didn't have a choice, I agreed. "Okay."

He started writing.

I forced myself to say the next words. "And what if I lose?"

Laying the pen on the table next to the pad of paper, he gave a casual shrug. "I'm not sure what I want to bet yet. So, for right now, we'll just keep track of who's winning or losing and then we'll tally it up at the end. Five games for five days at camp. Sound good?"

I swallowed and nodded.

"Stop looking at me like that," he snapped. "We're just having a little damn fun."

I lowered my eyes. "Can I trade some cards now?"

"Yup. Go ahead."

Pulling the queen, the five, and the eight from my hand, I laid them in the discard pile. Mr. Phillips dealt me three new cards and I picked them up. Another queen, an ace, and a three. I tried not to let the disappointment show on my face, but I could tell from the excitement in his eyes that I wasn't very successful.

Pulling out one card, Mr. Phillips laid it on the table and dealt himself a new one. "Normally, we would bet again now," he said. "But since we're playing for our own special arrangement, we'll keep it at one day."

My tongue felt so thick in my mouth I could barely speak around it. "Okay."

"All right, let's see what you've got."

I laid my hand down on the table, face up.

"A pair," he announced. Then he shook his head. "It's not impossible to win with only one pair, but it's not often that it happens." He laid his cards out. "What I have is a flush. See how they're all the same suit?" He pointed to the heart beneath the number on one of the cards. "A flush beats a pair."

My shoulders sagged in defeat, and my eyes burned with tears at the unjustness of it all. His eyes hardened at my reaction, but I wouldn't give him the satisfaction of seeing me cry.

"I'll tell you what." He paused. Probably waiting for me to look at him. But I couldn't. Not yet. After a few pounding beats of my heart, he continued. "I'll go ahead and give you a chance to win that day back. I think it's only fair since you're so new at this. How does that sound? Luna?"

I blinked away the last of the tears and lifted my chin.

"How does that sound?" he repeated.

"I would appreciate that," I managed to say. "Thank you."

I lost seven out of ten games that night. Mr. Phillips decided his bet was for me to sit on his lap and kiss him on the lips. And I did. Because I had agreed to play, win or lose.

Later, instead of doing homework, I got on my cheap laptop and researched how to play poker.

We played at least two or three times a week, but it took me a long time to get good enough to beat Mr. Phillips. As soon as I started to gain the upper hand, he would change the game. I learned how to play five-card draw, Texas hold 'em, and seven-card stud. The things we bet on started out simple enough. I would bet something Logan needed money for. If I won, Mr. Phillips would strike that particular thing off of his list of things I owed him for. If I lost, I paid him by doing something he wanted.

I stopped asking for anything for myself.

It started out simple. A kiss on the cheek or the mouth. Allowing him to buy me clothes that showed off my body more and wearing them for him. Sitting on his lap while we watched something on television.

I sat very still when on his lap. If I moved at all, he'd get harder and harder beneath my rear end. Sometimes, though, he'd ask me to lean forward and grab his beer off the coffee table where he'd left it on purpose. He'd moan when I did, pushing up with his hips, only to take the bottle from me and set it on the end table beside him without even taking a drink.

Eventually, it progressed into more. He would want to touch my breasts or between my legs. Over my clothes at first, but the more I lost the games, the more intimate our encounters became.

Then, he had me touch him.

A month before I turned sixteen, my foster father took my virginity. He wasn't gentle, and he left a lot of bruises on my pale skin that I had to cover up with long sleeves, pants, and makeup so Logan wouldn't see them and do something stupid. My brother might've been four years younger, but he was super protective of me, and I wouldn't have put it past him to try to protect my honor or some such bullshit. Which only would've gotten him hurt. Or, at the very least, had us thrown back into the system, and possibly separated from each other.

Mr. Phillips had also put me on birth control and supplied me with condoms to protect me from STDs. So, there was that, at least.

Of course, he was only protecting his new investment. Now that he'd personally popped my cherry, he planned to monetize my body and my newly acquired poker skills.

So, I guess I could say he taught me everything I knew.

CHAPTER 4

Luna

Now

I fought to turn my head, sucking in a much-needed breath as soon as I was able to get my face free of the comforter. My room reeked of the alcohol seeping from Gino's pores. A smell that was familiar to me, and almost comforting by now. Men who drank too much were men who did stupid things—like spend all of their money just to watch me get naked.

Opening my eyes, I saw movement in the darkness outside my window...a man standing in the shadows of the large oak tree.

One of Gino's guards peeping in at us, I was sure. I should've been mortified. I should've felt ashamed. But I felt absolutely nothing as he turned and walked away. After all, by now all of his men—and most of the people at the wedding today—knew how I'd ended up here.

I'd bet it all and lost to the old Italian capo whose fat stomach was currently pressing me down into the mattress. It was so large I didn't know how he found his dick to ram it into me. Yet he managed somehow, because he was currently plowing my unprepared vagina from behind, cursing because I wasn't wet and ready for him.

So no, I didn't feel any of those things. I only felt angry.

The thing was, it wasn't directed toward the man behind me. Or the one outside who'd just watched me trying to fight off my new "owner" without doing a damn thing to help me. No, the anger was directed only at myself, because I had no one else to blame for this predicament.

Just me.

In a desperate attempt to distract myself from what was happening, I let my mind wander, distancing myself from the sound of skin slapping on skin and the feel of Gino's pudgy fingers digging into my hips as he fought to breathe. I'd gotten pretty good at doing this over the years. My body's been the main moneymaker for me and —unbeknownst to him—my younger brother since I was fifteen, when I first discovered that men would pay for the opportunity to touch my blossoming curves. Thanks to my foster father and, eventually, his friends.

When I was eighteen, I started dancing at a strip club and moved my brother and me out of our last foster home with an advance on my first paycheck. Our foster parents didn't fight me about leaving. And once I was old enough to move out and would no longer be there to be his whore, Mr. Phillips had no incentive to keep Logan there.

I liked dancing. It paid a hell of a lot better, and I didn't have to let the customers fuck me. Not unless I wanted them to because I needed the influx of cash. And, sometimes, I did. Especially when the rent was due, or my brother Logan needed books for school, or if his financial aid was late hitting his account. At those times, I did whatever I had to do to make sure he stayed in school. My life might be fucked up after the way we'd grown up, but I refused to allow his to be. My little brother was going to finish his degree, get a great job, and live his best fucking life if it killed me.

So, I did what I had to do. But this time, it was *my* choice. No one forced me to do anything, either. The club I worked at now was a decent place. The bodyguards watched out for us, and we didn't have to share our earnings with anyone. Everyone from the manager to the busboy was paid very well.

My best-earning nights, however, were actually Thursday nights. Not because we had more customers than usual, but because on Thursday nights the club owner opened up the secret back room where the high-stakes poker games took place. On those nights, my tips nearly tripled.

For the first few months, I worked the private room strictly as one of the "girls." Our job was to look pretty, keep our mouths shut, and bring the players good luck. Sometimes, that meant sitting on one of their laps. Sometimes it meant serving them drinks and lighting whatever they were smoking. And we were always topless. Usually, it was the same group of guys. All dressed in suits. All very well-mannered with me and the other girls. Only a few of them ever stayed after the game for a little more intimate time with us.

Which gave me the perfect opportunity to observe the players.

Over time, I started to learn their tells. It was pretty easy since we were almost always in the room, and none of them bothered to hide their hands from us. I admit, it was stupid on their part, but not an oversight I was about to point out. Let them think we were all a bunch of brainless whores. Nothing but boobs and asses and pretty smiles.

Then one night when I was helping the busboys clean up after a late shift, I overheard Jeff, our manager, on the phone discussing a special game night for that coming Monday.

I set the dishes in the sink to be washed and wiped my hands on one of the dish towels. "Do you need any extra girls Monday?" I asked when he ended the call. "I could use a little extra cash this month and I'd be happy to work the game."

He shook his head. "Thanks, Luna. But there won't be any girls for this game. This is gonna be a high-stakes game with a few esteemed guests who'd rather their attendance here be kept on the down low."

I raised an eyebrow. "High-stakes? Then what the hell do you call the Thursday night games?" I'd watched tens of thousands of dollars get won and lost over and over again every week.

He smiled. "For those guys? That's what you call well-off businessmen with gambling problems. But for these guys coming Monday? Those Thursday night bets are nothing. Pocket change for fun with the boys and to get away from the wives for a night."

Pocket change. Ten-thousand-dollar bets were considered pocket change?

My mind started to spin. Imagine being in on a fucking game like that. If I won, I could set myself and Logan up for life.

My heart pounding in my throat, I asked, "Can I play?"

Jeff didn't react at first, then he barked out a laugh. "Good one, honey."

"I'm serious," I told him. "I know how to play. My...foster father was a big poker player, and he taught me when I was fifteen. I played against him and his friends for years."

He stared at me for a few seconds, and from the look on his face, I got the impression he wasn't sure whether or not to believe me.

"I'm not bullshitting you," I told him. "I can play. And I'm really good."

With a shake of his head, he said, "Nobody gets into these games without an invitation." When I continued to stare at him, he shrugged. "But a few of the guys know you from hanging out in the club, so let me ask. Maybe I can get you in on a Thursday game. I'm not making any promises here, though. So don't get your hopes up too much."

I gave him a big smile. "Thanks, Jeff. I appreciate it."

"But if they let you play, don't show these guys up too much, Luna bird. I doubt they'd handle losing to you very well. You know, with you being one of the girls and all."

"Got it."

And that's how I started playing with the boys. The following week, they greeted me at the first game with patronizing smiles and smug attitudes, their eyes wandering over my skimpy dancer costume that I purposely hadn't changed out of, hoping it would distract them. Or, at the very least, making me appear harmless. But by the third game, no one was looking at my boobs anymore. And the smug smiles had turned into flared nostrils and sharp looks. Heeding Jeff's advice, I threw the last game. I still came out ahead, but narrowing the gap between our winnings made them much more amiable.

Calling my winnings "beginner's luck," they invited me to the following week's game to give them a chance to win back what they'd lost. And the week after that. And the week after that. Until my reputation as a player made it around the club and into the ears of the Monday night players.

A month later, when my boss told me I'd been invited to sit at the table with the big boys, I was shocked. And terrified. So far, I'd won a nice little nest egg for me and Logan, but I'd need my entire life savings to play with these guys. With that kind of buy-in, I could lose everything I'd won with a couple of bad hands. These guys were in a completely different league than the guys I'd been playing with, and I honestly didn't know if I was good enough for a seat at their table. But damn, it was tempting.

Because all I kept thinking was, what if I won?

I chewed on the inside of my cheek as I considered their offer. A few games. That's all I needed. The winnings from a few weeks of playing and Logan and I would be set for life. No more worrying about rent, or college loans, or anything. Hell, I could quit dancing, and Logan could take his time finding a job after he graduated. We could travel, see the world, eat our way through France and Italy or wherever we wanted.

We could be truly free.

So, I showed up the following Monday. Right away I could tell the men at this table were different. Their suits were cut to perfection and had labels like Armani and Brioni. Their eyes were hard and scrutinizing as they checked their weapons at the door. They greeted each other in the traditional Italian manner with handshakes or hugs and a kiss on the cheek as they measured each other up.

I stood as they approached the table, unsure of what to do. I was met with cold stares and formal nods by all. These men weren't here to have a little fun. These men were serious.

And dangerous.

The first night, my heart raced so fast that I almost changed my mind and backed out. But somehow, I ended up sitting in one of the chairs, telling the guy across from me to deal me in. He eyed me hard, his stare almost disbelieving, and I had to resist the urge to get up and leave again.

"She's good," Jeff told him. "She was invited to play."

The guy holding the cards glanced at Jeff, then came back to me. "Gino," he introduced himself. Dragging his eyes away, he started dealing.

"Luna," I told him, discreetly wiping my sweaty palms on my dress pants. I'd worn my most professional outfit—black slacks and a cream-colored blouse that buttoned down the front. But I guess the clothes couldn't disguise the girl I really was.

"I know." My skin crawled as his eyes wandered over my chest. "We're not playing with tip money here, honey."

"I know," I threw back at him.

With a shrug, he picked up his hand.

My heart was about to gallop right out of my chest, but once the game started, my nerves settled, and I did what I did best—read the room and take their money. But even though it gave me a sense of satisfaction to lighten the pockets of these men in a way that involved using my brain instead of my body, I knew better than to get too smug.

I won more money that night than I'd ever seen in my life. The following week, I won even more. It was almost enough to quit my job. Almost, but not quite. I needed just a little bit more, and we'd be set for a long time. For life if I was smart and invested some of it.

But eventually, my luck had to run out. Which was precisely how I'd ended up in my current situation.

I'd had the hand to beat all hands, and I'd gotten a little too cocky at the poker table. Everyone else had bowed out. Everyone except Gino. And I'd been sure he was bluffing. So I'd bet it all. Everything I had. Just to stay in the game.

But the son of a bitch had fooled me, and I'd lost everything. *Everything.*

As I'd sat there staring at the cards on the table in disbelief, Gino had come back with a counteroffer. He would take my money—everything I had for Logan and me to survive and everything I'd managed to save—but only temporarily, if I would agree to be his companion for an undetermined amount of time.

Exclusively.

While I was his, he would cover all our bills, including Logan's college loans, free and clear. As for the money I'd just lost, he would put it away in an account, and when he was done with me, he'd give it back and set me free.

All I had to do was give him full use of my body whenever he wanted it. Sometimes he just wanted a pretty girl on his arm or a dinner companion, and on occasion he wanted to fuck. And in exchange, my little brother would be able to stay in college without being buried in debt when he graduated in two years. He could stay in the dorm, have a car, and concentrate on his studies without having to work part-time. Then, once he graduated, Gino promised he'd put in a good word for him with some people he knew.

How he knew about Logan, I didn't know. But, obviously, I wasn't the only one who'd done my research.

I wasn't a fool. I knew exactly who Gino was and who he associated with. I'd seen him plenty of times in the club, watching me dance, before we ever faced each other across the poker table. You didn't work a job like I did and not hear about your customers. Especially the ones who always seemed to have money to burn. So I'd known who he was and what he did for a living when I'd bet against him. I wasn't under any false impressions that I'd retain any freedom if I lost. He owned me now until he saw fit to let me go. If he ever did.

I sucked in a breath when a stinging slap landed on my bare ass, and I realized Gino had finished. I laid still, hoping he would leave so I could get up and go scrub the feel of him from my skin.

Still inside me, he struggled to catch his breath, adjusting his stance to get a better purchase on the hardwood floor. I felt him rapidly shrinking as he pulled most of the way out of me and then tried to push his way back in. But his now flaccid penis was done for the night. He sniffed loudly and squeezed my ass, then backed away from me. But I could still feel the weight of his stare.

His voice was gruff when he said, "Go get cleaned up."

Without looking at him, I pushed myself up off the bed and pulled the skirt of my dress down to cover my nakedness. Then I went to the bathroom and gratefully closed the door. I started the shower, knowing he'd be gone by the time I finished.

This was the way it had been with us since he'd brought me to live here. During the day, I was left to my own devices as long as I didn't leave the house without his permission. Every night, we would have dinner together either here at the house or at an expensive restaurant, and he would tell me stories about his life. Which, I had to admit, made me kind of nervous. There were definitely things I was better off not knowing about his line of work.

Sometimes, though, he would talk to me like I'd been there when these things happened. Or like I should know the people he spoke of. It was weird, but he *was* getting up there in years. I thought maybe he was starting to lose it in his old age, so I just went along with him because if I pointed out that I had no idea what he was talking about, he'd stop laughing and joking and fall into this weird mood that I couldn't pull him out of, and he'd send me to my room still hungry.

After dinner, he'd head out to go do...I had no idea what. Most nights, I'd end up back in my room alone. But sometimes, like tonight, dinner would end with me bent over something while he rammed me from behind. On those nights, he'd study me for a long time with this strange look on his face I couldn't read. Sometimes, he'd talk, but more often than not, he'd clam up and grow moody instead. Always on the nights he was drinking. I knew it even if I wasn't with him because I'd smell the booze on his breath.

This was the first time he'd gotten that rough with me, though.

The accusation he'd made after practically breaking down my bedroom door came back to me.

Bet you liked all the attention you got tonight in that dress, didn't you?

I frowned, still wondering where that had come from. Hardly anyone had given me a second glance. No one except Tristan, the guy who'd been forced to babysit me while Gino went to talk to Luca. And I would hardly call the way he stared at me sexual.

You think you can just leave me? Is that what you think?

It was pure rage, not the haze of alcohol, that had darkened his eyes when he'd thrown me into the window.

Blinking back tears of pain and humiliation, I scrubbed myself clean, ignoring the tender spots that would surely be bruises by tomorrow. When I came out of the bathroom, as predicted, Gino was gone. So I curled up in bed and went to sleep, trying not to think about what had happened tonight, and hoping this wasn't going to be what my life would become.

When I got up the next morning, a covered tray was on the dresser. My stomach growled as I lifted the lid to find a hunk of bread and a glass of water.

What the hell was this?

Ignoring my aching bladder, I hurried over to the bedroom door and tried the knob. It was locked. I banged on it with my closed fist. "Gino! Open this door!"

Of course, there was no answer. I pressed my ear to the wood and listened. Nothing. Not so much as the scuff of a shoe on the floor. Closing my eyes, I pressed my forehead against it.

I had no idea what I'd done to deserve this. And if I were a smart woman, I would beg his forgiveness for whatever supposed infraction had made him lock me in here.

But, apparently, I was not a smart woman. I was a stubborn one. And one of these days—probably when I was nothing but skin and bones and too fragile to walk across the room—I would regret not swallowing my pride.

However, today was not that day.

Neither was the next.

There were no more dinners. No more anything. Just me in my bedroom with nothing to do but look out the window and wait for the occasional hunk of bread and glass of water.

By the third day alone in this room, being fed just enough to keep me alive, I was starting to fucking think about it. I rolled over on the bed, ignoring the tears gathering in my eyes as I stared at the door, willing Gino to walk through it with a four-course dinner for me. Of course, he didn't.

The fucker had even taken my cell phone away, my only connection to my brother.

I was a prisoner.

CHAPTER 5

Tristan

"What did you do, Tristan?"

Luca stared at me across the floor of his office. He'd just poured himself a generous dram of whiskey and still held the full glass in his hand.

"Which time?" I asked him. If I was about to confess to something, I wanted to ensure it was the correct thing. Otherwise, my rule was what Luca didn't know wouldn't hurt him. And there were quite a few things Luca—and even Enzo—didn't know.

"At Gino's. Last night. One of his guards is missing. You went there against my orders, didn't you?"

I folded my jacket and draped it over the end of the couch in front of his desk. Then I slid my hands into the front pockets of my black slacks. "Mmm. That."

"Yes, *that*." He raised one eyebrow at me and waited.

"He won't be found. I called Milo, and he took care of it." Milo was excellent at his job. He could clean up a body spread out for a quarter mile and the cops wouldn't find a scrap of DNA. He was also good at keeping secrets. I had no idea what the other guards, such as they were, had told Gino about their missing friend. Nor did I care. It wouldn't be connected to me or Luca, so it was no longer my problem.

He stared at me for a long moment. Then, he sighed. "Well, there's that, at least." Finishing off what was in his glass, he poured himself another. "May I ask *why* you felt the need to kill one of Gino's guards?"

"He got in my way. And I thought it best if I didn't leave any witnesses."

He rubbed his temple. "And why were you on Gino's property?"

I briefly considered lying, but I quickly realized there would be no point. "I think you and I both know the answer to that question."

His movements were unhurried, the set of his shoulders relaxed, but he didn't fool me. He was upset. "You're right. I do know. Did she see you? Or any of Gino's men? Other than the obvious one, of course."

"No."

"What did you do while you were there?"

I hesitated, unwilling to divulge any more information than I had to. "I watched her."

"That's all?"

"Yes."

His eyes narrowed on me.

"I know you told me to leave her alone—"

"I did," he agreed as he strode back to his desk, whiskey glass in hand.

"—but I can't," I finished.

"And why can't you?"

I thought about that for a moment. "I don't know."

Setting his glass down, he sat and leaned back in his seat, rubbing his forehead with the fingers of one hand. He was losing patience with me.

"I'm sorry," I told him.

"No," he said. "You're not. But I'm just trying to understand here, T."

How could I explain something to him I didn't understand myself? "I'm sorry," I repeated. "I don't have an answer for you."

He sighed heavily, and his eyes caught mine and held. "You told me at the wedding that you thought you knew her from somewhere."

"Yes." It wasn't a lie. She did seem familiar to me.

Eyes going to his computer monitor, he typed in his password and pulled up a screen. "Since you've been so busy stalking the girl, I've been doing a little digging."

I walked around his desk, standing beside him so I could see the screen, and watched as he opened an email. My eyes immediately locked onto the picture in the body of the email. And for a moment, I forgot how to breathe. Luna's name appeared in bold across the top of a current photo of her. It looked like a license or passport photo from the look of the plain background. But even with bright lights and no filters, she was stunning. As I stared at the image, my heart began to pound heavily in my chest, and my skin grew clammy underneath my suit. A sense of desperation rushed through me to be near her, throwing me off balance. To make sure she was okay after what I'd witnessed the night before. Forcing myself to focus on what Luca was showing me, I shook off the feeling.

Further down in the email was another name and another image. A guy somewhere around her age. First name Logan. Same last name.

A flash of heat burst inside of me, and my fists clenched at my sides. Was she married? Did she have a husband somewhere wondering where she was? A husband who had a much bigger claim on her than some old, Italian capo?

"Luna Marie Wilde," Luca read. "Twenty-six years old. Single."

The room tilted around me, and I took a breath, bringing it back into focus. It shouldn't bother me so much to think of her as someone's wife when she was currently Gino's whore. It just seemed...different somehow.

"Up until two weeks ago, she was a dancer at Honey's, the strip club in north Austin that Gino has recently taken over for me."

"I know the place." I'd gone there once or twice to collect Luca's share of the nightly profits when his usual runner wasn't available. The club also contained a secret room in the back for gambling.

The copper taste of blood filled my mouth as I bit down on the inside of my cheek, thinking about Luna stripping for the type of men that frequented Honey's. Had I ever seen her there? No. I couldn't have. She definitely would've caught my attention. Just thinking about her on that stage made me want to punch something.

"Logan is her younger brother," he continued, distracting me from the black hole I was about to spiral down. "Four-year difference between them. He attends UT Dallas and is currently there for spring semester classes. In the fall, he'll be starting his junior year. On his breaks, he lives with her." He scrolled down. "They were raised together in foster homes until Luna turned eighteen and petitioned the courts for custody of her brother and got it." He looked up at me. "Any of this sound familiar?"

I shook my head. "No." Bracing my weight with one hand on his desk, I leaned down and read more of the report, careful to keep plenty of space between Luca and myself. I didn't really worry about him touching me, accidentally or otherwise, but I'd kept the habit for so long it was second nature now.

Scanning the rest of the email, I chewed the inside of my lower lip. Nothing stood out to me. "Was her name always 'Wilde'?"

"If it was something different when she was younger, there's no record of it here."

Straightening, I crossed my arms over my chest.

"I can ask around more," Luca told me. "But I don't know that we'll find anything else. It seems like she was a typical kid in the system who got out and ended up doing sex work like many of them do. I don't think there's any other way you would've run across her. Perhaps you saw her dancing, and that's why she seems familiar."

"Maybe," I agreed, although I already knew that wasn't it. It was more than that. I would've remembered her if it was only a matter of her tits catching my eye.

Luca shut down his email and turned his chair until he was facing me. "I must repeat my original order, Tristan. Stay away from the girl. She's nothing to you. And pursuing this strange obsession you seem to have will only cause us a shit ton of problems that I really don't need right now."

"*Capisco*," I told him. I understand. And I did. I understood why Luca gave out orders, and why we needed to obey them. I always obeyed him. He could completely depend on me.

But not this time.

THAT NIGHT, I returned to Gino's and watched Luna through her bedroom window. Something was wrong.

Luna—dressed in sweatpants and a T-shirt—paced the room with long, angry strides, her arms stiff at her sides and her hands clenched into fists. When she shoved her hair back off her face, I saw her eyes were bright with unshed tears. She stopped short in front of the door and banged on it, screaming for Gino, for anyone. Gripping the doorknob, her entire body strained with the effort to turn it, but nothing happened. She gave the door a final slap before dropping her forehead to rest on the wood.

My cell phone vibrated in my pants pocket. It was a text from Luca, wondering if I'd made it to the drop-off location yet, where I was meeting with his contact from the cartel. I shot off a text letting him know I'd be there on time. When I was finished, Luna had gone back to pacing. Quickly and quietly, I made my way back out to the road where I'd left the SUV.

For the next few nights, I watched her from outside her window. Her behavior didn't change much, although as the days went by her actions became more and more lethargic. She looked...fragile. Weak. By the third night, her hair had lost its shine and there were bags under her eyes that hadn't been there before. Her skin was pale. She was still beautiful to me, just muted somehow. Tired.

Staying in the shadows, I crept closer. Her door suddenly opened and two guards entered her room. I recognized them as the two who were always closest to Gino. One of them grabbed Luna as she made a rush for the door, wrapping his arms around her from behind and lifting her until her bare feet kicked nothing but air. The other set a covered tray and a glass of water on the dresser and walked back out of the room. As soon as he was out, the one holding her threw her onto the bed and left the room, slamming the door in her face when she scrambled to reach it.

She slammed both hands against the door, then rushed to the tray. Lifting the lid and dropping it on the floor, she picked up a piece of bread and tore into it. There was nothing else on the tray.

Gino was fucking starving her.

My upper lip lifted in a snarl as my stomach remembered the long-ago ache of hunger pains. I didn't want her to feel that pain. And I didn't want her thinner. She was perfect just the way she was. Whatever offense she'd made to make him punish her this way, it couldn't be so bad that she deserved to be locked in her room and starved.

If Gino wasn't going to feed her properly, I would bring her something to eat.

Luna stopped eating suddenly, and her head whipped toward the door. Setting the last bite of bread back on the tray, she turned to face it. The door opened, and Gino filled the frame, body blocking the exit like he was afraid she'd squeeze by him and bolt. His eyes raked down her body briefly before sweeping around the room. I withdrew deeper into the shadows of the tall bushes beside her window, obstructing my view of Luna, but Gino was the one I needed to keep eyes on now.

"I just found out I need to go to a dinner tonight," he announced. "If you think you can stop all of this racket and behave yourself, I'll bring you with me."

"Will I be allowed to eat something besides bread?" she asked.

"I might let you have a salad. As long as you smile and don't start any shit."

Was he being serious? She clearly needed more to eat than a salad.

"I can do that," she said after a moment, her tone hard to decipher, but definitely not the confident voice of the woman I met at the wedding. I didn't like this new, meek

Luna. My hand went to my gun, but before I could do anything, Gino spoke again.

"Good," he said. "Get cleaned up and meet me in the entry in thirty minutes. Do not be late." He went to leave, then stopped and turned back to her. "Wear the blue dress. The one that matches your eyes. You know the one I like."

"I need to shower, but I'll be ready."

Satisfied, Gino left, closing the door behind him.

Luna appeared in my line of vision as she walked over to the door, opened it, and shut it again, testing the lock. Then she disappeared from my view again. Seconds later, I heard the shower come on.

While she got ready, I checked the window to see if it was wired to a security system. There were no visible magnets or transmitters, and the frame looked old. Out of curiosity, I pulled the screen off and hid it behind one of the bushes. Then I tested the window. The lock was an old-fashioned mechanism that wiggled when I tried to raise the window. Glancing behind me to confirm none of the guards had wandered over this way, I braced my palms on the glass and shoved upward.

The lock moved, but it wasn't quite enough to break it.

Pulling a knife out of the pocket of my black cargo pants, I jimmied it under the frame between the upper and lower panes and managed to move the latch into the unlocked position. I put my knife away, placed my palms on the glass again, and shoved upward. This time, it moved.

Raising it a few inches, I waited, listening. The shower was still running, but I didn't hear anything else. Seconds ticked by. When no guards came running into the room to investigate, I opened it all the way and crawled inside, leaving the window open, just in case I had to make a quick escape.

The room smelled like Luna. I closed my eyes as I inhaled deep. Walking over to the bed, I picked up her pillow and pressed it to my face, breathing her in. It smelled like her shampoo. Pantene, if I wasn't mistaken. I remembered the scent from Enzo's wedding when she'd swung her head around to talk to me and all that long, dark hair had tumbled over her shoulder and down her back. I clenched the pillow in my fists, wishing I could feel her hair.

Something tickled my face. Putting the pillow down, I ran my hand over it again and came back with a few strands of her hair. I wrapped them around my index finger and rubbed them with my thumb. Soft. Like I knew they would be. Grabbing a tissue from the box on the nightstand, I carefully folded it around the strands and put it in my pocket.

I walked over to the closet, my boots silent on the ugly green and white area rug covering the wood floors. It matched the comforter on the bed, but that was about all that could be said for it. Both were ugly, and unsuitable for a woman as radiant as Luna.

A variety of dresses and shoes, all high-heeled, filled the closet. I scanned the clothes until I found the blue dress Gino must've been talking about. But he was wrong. It wasn't the same color as her eyes. This dress was bland. The color muted. Luna's eyes were luminous, a multi-dimensional cobalt blue edged with a ring of black. I could stare into her eyes forever.

I took the dress from its spot and hung it at the front of the row, then crept back into the bedroom. In the top drawer of her dresser, I found all manner of silky things and a few more sensible cotton items. I picked up one of each and decided I preferred the cotton. They seemed more real. More like her. The silk was something she wore when she was pretending to be someone she wasn't.

Remembering the hamper I'd seen in the closet, I returned to it, plucked out a pair of striped cotton underwear, and brought them to my face. The warm, sweet smell of Luna filled my nose and sent blood rushing to my cock. I groaned aloud, crumpling them up and shoving them into the front pocket of my pants.

The water was still running, but she would probably be done soon. I should leave. Yet I couldn't make myself go. Not yet. Instead, I went over to the bathroom door and carefully turned the knob. The slight creak of the door was disguised by the sound of the fan as I cracked it open and peered inside.

In the mirror, I could see Luna through the clear glass door of the shower. My heart stuttered in my chest, and for a moment, I wondered if I'd ever be able to breathe again. Swallowing hard, I drank in the perfection of her body as she closed her eyes and raised her arms over her head to rinse her long hair. Milky, pale skin contrasted with her black hair. Her nipples matched the color of her lips. The alluring shadow of hair between her legs made it clear she didn't shave or wax herself bare. Good. I wasn't into little girls. I liked women to look like women.

Would the hair there be as soft as the hair on her head? I'd never touched a woman intimately, so I had no idea what to expect. I'd never even been curious before. But with Luna, I was desperate to know.

She finished rinsing her hair and turned around, shutting off the water. I allowed myself a quick glance at the graceful length of her back, the curve of her hips, and the roundness of her ass before I slowly eased the door shut again.

I stood staring at the white wood in front of me, breathing through my mouth as I listened to her dry herself off. Forcing myself to move, I went back out the window and carefully closed it.

But I didn't leave.

Instead, I waited, watching through the window from the shadows. A few minutes later, she came out wrapped in a towel. Her hair was dry and pulled back into a simple ponytail, and makeup brightened her eyes and lips. Makeup she didn't need to look beautiful. A picture of her face with her lipstick smeared and mascara running down her cheeks made my already hard cock painfully swollen. She grabbed some underthings from the top drawer of the dresser—silky ones—and disappeared into the closet. I smiled when she came out wearing the required blue dress and heels.

Back in the bedroom, she stopped, looking around, her expression anxious yet resigned. I shrank back out of view when her eyes skimmed over the window. With a slight frown, she reached just inside the closet door and pulled out a small purse with a long strap. Holding it in her hand, she schooled her expression, lifting her chin and setting her shoulders before leaving the room, pulling the door closed behind her.

Once I was sure she was gone, I returned the screen to the window and made my way back to the car I'd left parked about a half a mile down the road, easily evading Gino's guards.

Tomorrow.

I would see her again tomorrow.

Tonight, I would just leave her a gift. One I think she'd appreciate.

CHAPTER 6

Luna

At dinner that night, I was the epitome of a loving girlfriend, gushing over everything Gino said and laughing at all of his stupid jokes without interrupting their conversation. But judging by the looks he began sending my way, I might have overplayed my role just a bit.

As the waiter was getting everyone's order, Gino took the opportunity to tell me, "You're not fooling anyone, girl. So just sit there and shut up and look pretty. I didn't bring you here so you could run your fucking mouth."

Heat flooded my face, and I leaned toward him so only he would hear. "If I'm off my game, it's because I'm fucking starving. You promised me some food. Real food."

I had his attention now. "So I did," he finally admitted. My stomach caved in on itself with hunger as he raised his hand to signal the waiter. "I forgot to order a side salad for my companion, please. Italian dressing. Yes, that's all."

Holy shit. He'd been serious before. A salad. He'd ordered me a fucking salad. And not even a large dinner salad with chicken and bread. A fucking *side* salad. Gino threw around threats all the time. They rarely stuck, especially with me, and I was really hoping that this dinner was his way of apologizing for his treatment of me the last few days.

Guess I was wrong.

I almost broke down and cried right there in the middle of the restaurant. He didn't feel bad at all about what had happened. He wasn't trying to make up with me. This was just another way for him to torture me.

Gino's two sons, Gildo and Salvatore, sat across from us, along with the guests of honor, two of the Irish. From what I could gather of the conversation so far, Salvatore had offended the Irishmen somehow, and Gino was still trying to make nice. It made sense that Salvatore would be the one to go off and do whatever the fuck he wanted, because of the two men Gino had somehow managed to spurt from his loins, Salvatore was definitely the more dangerous of the two. And he hated the Irish. Living in Gino's house, I'd picked up on that real quick. Even sitting across from him at dinner, I could feel the dangerous vibe that pulsed from him in icy waves and made gooseflesh rise on my arms. A warning that any and all would be smart to heed.

As if he sensed my attention, those cold, bright, hazel eyes met mine across the table. "Don't you want more than a salad, *bella*?"

God, yes, I did. I opened my mouth to say as much when I felt Gino's hand squeeze my leg in warning. He glared at his son but said nothing. This left me with two choices: I could ignore him and order more food, thereby appeasing my immediate need of being hungry, knowing there'd be more punishment waiting for me when we got home. Or, I could continue to starve and hope my suffering would please him enough that he wouldn't lock me in my room again.

I opted for the second choice. "No," I said with a smile. "I'm actually not very hungry." My stomach twisted and moaned in protest. "A salad will be perfect."

Gino's hand left my thigh as I fought to keep the smile on my face under Salvatore's sharp stare. He shifted his gaze to his father. Then, with a small, uncaring shrug, turned his attention back to the conversation with the Irish, his expression giving nothing away.

No longer the subject of his rapt attention, I released my breath and relaxed just a bit. I didn't fool myself into thinking either of Gino's sons gave a crap about me, and honestly, I was surprised he'd even noticed what his father had ordered for me. So it was stupid of me to wish he would've pushed the subject more and insisted I get something else. Yet, somehow, disappointment still weighed me down.

When my salad finally came, it took everything I had not to bend over the table and just start wolfing it down like a dog. I'd never been a big vegetable eater, but I was so sick of bread and water I'd take just about anything at this moment.

My eyes lingered on my plate as the waiter carried it away, my only consolation that their meals would be out soon and I wouldn't have to sit here much longer. But I was so, so wrong. Gino made me stay at the table for another two hours while he, his sons, and the Irishmen ate course after course of delicious smelling food and discussed whatever the hell they were talking about. I was too hungry to pay much attention. He even ordered dessert.

The fucking bastard.

On the ride home, I sat silent and sullen, the salad I'd eaten gurgling in my stomach as my digestive system struggled to process the shock of having something besides yeast and water.

Gino sat just as silent and brooding as I was, staring out the other window. Obviously, whatever he'd been expecting to accomplish with this dinner hadn't gone as he'd planned.

But that wasn't my problem. "Can I have my cell phone back?"

At first, I thought he was going to ignore me, but then he turned to me with a frown.

"If I don't call Logan soon, he'll start to worry. And…" I took a breath and pushed my luck, "I think that's the least I deserve after tonight."

His eyes narrowed and he sniffed obnoxiously, but he didn't argue with me. Gino wasn't an evil man, not completely. He was impatient and entitled. But he wasn't a complete monster.

I softened my voice. "Please, Gino. I don't want him to worry."

Grudgingly, he reached into the inside pocket of his suit jacket, pulled out my cell, and handed it to me.

"Thank you," I told him.

With a grunt, he turned back to the window.

I tapped the screen to check for messages, but nothing happened. Pressing the power button on the side, I prayed the battery wasn't dead, that Gino had only shut it off. I smiled when the white apple appeared on the screen and the phone powered up. It was still at forty-seven percent battery.

There was only one missed message from Logan, just checking in. I texted him back, apologizing for not responding before now and letting him know I'd call him as soon as I could. He responded with an emoji face, one eyebrow lifted, and a thumbs up.

When we arrived home, Gino barely looked at me as he left me at the door to my room, shutting and locking it behind me without a word. Raising my fist to pound on the door, obscenities forming on my tongue, I froze, distracted by the most wonderfully delicious smell coming from...inside my room!

Spinning around, I spotted a Tupperware container on the dresser and nearly sprinted over to it. Had Gino only been fucking with me after all and had his chef leave me dinner? Or was it someone else?

I stared at the container like there was a snake hidden inside. What if it was the guard who'd watched us through the window the other night? Or what if that hadn't been a guard at all? What if it had been Salvatore, Gino's son? He was the only one who'd seemed to notice that I'd hardly eaten tonight. But he'd left the restaurant at the same time we had, so how the hell would he have managed to have dinner waiting for me inside my room? He'd never left the table all night, and I never noticed him pull his phone out to text anyone...

Deciding I was too hungry to care, I tore off the lid. Inside was a chicken breast with some kind of cream sauce and a side of potatoes. No veggies.

Salivating, I used my fingers to pick up the entire chicken breast, ignoring the silver utensils wrapped in a cloth napkin, and stuffed it into my mouth. It was tender, seasoned to perfection, and filled with cheese and... spinach, maybe? And it was the best thing I'd ever tasted in my life.

I scarfed down the entire meal in less than five minutes flat, licking my fingers clean, and immediately regretted my decision when my stomach protested violently and sent me running to the bathroom. I cried as it all came back up. What was this new hell? Was Gino trying to poison me now?

My god. What if I'd eaten poisoned food? Panic quickened my breath, making my face hot. Gino was mafia. He must have enemies. What if someone was trying to get to him by hurting me, not knowing that losing me wouldn't be any great emotional loss for him?

After evacuating everything I'd just eaten, I flushed the toilet and rinsed my mouth. Then I sat on the side of the tub, dropped my head in my hands, and allowed myself a good thirty minutes to do nothing but feel sorry for myself.

"Okay," I said to myself between sobs. "Just calm down. You threw it all up. If the food was poisoned, you'd be on the floor by now."

By the time I was all cried out, my heart rate had slowed and my nerves had settled. I stripped out of my dress, silky underwear, and heels, washed my face, brushed my teeth, and brushed out my hair. Naked and not giving a shit who saw me, I walked to the dresser and found my favorite comfy nightshirt—soft gray cotton with a sleeping moon on the front. Pulling it over my head, I crawled into bed. Stomach cramping, I laid there in misery until I passed out with the light still on.

The next morning, the container was gone. In its place was another one that looked much the same and smelled faintly of eggs.

My stomach practically jumped out of my throat to get to them.

Running into the bathroom, I took care of my most urgent needs as fast as I could, and then I grabbed the container off the dresser, sat down right there on the floor, and ripped it open. I was right about the eggs. But they weren't just any old eggs. These had green onions, tomatoes, cheese, and some kind of other seasonings I'd never smelled before.

There was also a fresh bagel and soft cream cheese mixed with honey.

Weighing my options, I started with the bagel, figuring it would be the safer choice. Despite my hunger, I forced myself to take only three small bites and not shove it all down my throat like I had last night, giving my stomach time to accept the food. And to see if it was poisoned.

When nothing happened, I took a few more. Then I tried the eggs.

To my surprise, I could only eat half of it. With a sound of disappointment, I snapped the top back onto the container and wrapped up the rest of the bagel to save for a little later, stashing it all in the bottom drawer of the dresser so no one would sneak in and take it. The eggs were still warm, so I figured they'd be okay sitting out for another hour or so. Then I sat there waiting to see if my stomach was going to revolt or not. It was a little touch and go at first, but I managed to keep down my breakfast.

After about an hour, I finished the meal, even though I wasn't actually hungry. Just in case. I couldn't let it sit there and go bad, not when I didn't know if or when there would be more.

Hiding the empty container in the dresser, I found a pair of black, wide-leg yoga pants and a soft blue T-shirt with horizontal white stripes and took them with me into the bathroom to take another shower. I didn't really need it, but it was something to pass the time.

When I came out, Gino was standing in the middle of the room. Nervously, I glanced toward the dresser and the hidden container. I should've rinsed it out. Could he smell the food? Hopefully not.

"Luca is coming over," he said when I gave him a questioning look. "And Betta had to take the day off for some kind of family thing. I need you to come out and serve us lunch while he's here."

"Of course," I told him. Looking down at myself, I added. "I should change."

Gino gave me a cursory glance. "You're fine. It's nothing formal." He caught my bare feet. "Just put on some shoes and go on down to the kitchen. They'll be here in about thirty minutes."

Nothing like giving me some notice. But all I said was, "Okay."

He turned on his heel and left without saying anything else, leaving my door open behind him.

Freedom!

Sort of. I was still stuck in the house, but after spending weeks locked in my room, I felt like I was about to go to Disney World.

I slid on my most comfy slip-on shoes, grabbed the bag with the empty container inside, and practically skipped to the kitchen. The chef—I had no idea what her name was—was busy whipping up lunch. No sandwiches and chips for Gino and his guests. Oh, no. She was cooking risotto with veal, maybe? And a fancy salad. "Need some help?" I asked her.

"If you could go get the wine from the storeroom," she said. "I've already picked it out. Mr. Ricci prefers the chardonnay with his veal. Top shelf. Third over from the left."

"Got it." Hurrying down to the storeroom, I found the wine. "That smells wonderful," I told the chef when I returned. I wished I knew her name. Gino had just introduced her as "the chef" when I'd first arrived. And it seemed weird to ask her now. She was always very nice, though. However, I didn't think she was stupid enough to risk her job—or possibly her life—by sneaking me food. But it had to be someone in the house.

"Thank you," she said with a smile. "Mr. Luca is a very important guest. He gets only the best."

A thought occurred to me. "What did you make last night?"

"Last night?"

I nodded.

She thought about it for a second. "Oh! I made Mr. Ricci's favorite, gnocchi pasta with clams."

"No chicken?"

She shook her head. "Mr. Ricci isn't a huge fan of chicken. I hardly ever make it."

Shit.

"Does anyone else in the house ever cook?"

This time, she glanced at me, her brow furrowed. "No. I'm the only one who cooks. Mr. Ricci doesn't trust anyone else with his food. Why do you ask?"

I shook my head and widened my eyes to look innocent. "No reason. I was just wondering. The food is always so good."

Placated, she went back to her lunch preparations. "Thank you," she told me. "I was trained by the best chefs in Italy."

More puzzled than ever, I got out the wine glasses and silverware. I'd just opened the wine to let it breathe when the doorbell rang.

"Would you get that, please?"

"Sure," I told her. It occurred to me that she probably didn't know my name either. And maybe it was better that way.

That feeling of foreboding returned as I opened the front door and greeted the mafia boss and his men.

CHAPTER 7

Tristan

My breath caught and my heart fluttered within my chest when she opened the door.

Luna was stunning. Even more so than I remembered.

I stood on the stoop beside Enzo as we protected Luca's back, frozen in place as she greeted our boss with a nervous smile and offered to escort us to the formal dining room. We knew the way. We'd been here numerous times before. However, Gino always liked to put on a grand show of Luca's arrival, like he was some sort of royalty. Which, I guess, in the world of *La Cosa Nostra*, he was.

Instead of watching for threats, my eyes were glued to her rounded ass in those tight-knit pants as she led the way down the long hallway and into the heart of Gino's home.

Her long hair hung freely down her back, swishing back and forth with every sway of her hips, and I had to clench my fists at my sides to keep from shoving Luca out of the way and tangling my fingers in it. She glanced down a separate hallway, presenting us with her elegant profile for only a matter of seconds before she faced forward again. Was it my imagination, or did she look better today? There appeared to be more color in her cheeks, and the desperation was gone from her eyes, at least.

I was...disconcerted when she left us with Gino, softly closing the door behind her. I almost followed her before I remembered where I was and why. Still, it took me a minute to get my head back into the game.

Gino stood when we entered, showing his respect, and gave Luca his customary greeting by kissing him on both cheeks before nodding hello to Enzo and me. Surprisingly, he was alone in the room, but his men had to be lurking about somewhere, ready to jump us at a moment's notice if needed. Either that, or he was even more *scemo*—stupid—than I thought.

Gesturing to the chair on his right, he invited Luca to sit with him. I took my position behind our boss, against the wall and away from the windows, as did Enzo. We wouldn't be enjoying the meal. We were here solely to make sure Gino didn't start any shit.

Luna returned with a bottle of red wine and two wine glasses. She poured a taste for Luca to approve, then filled his glass before serving Gino. The muscles in Gino's jowls jumped as he ground his teeth, but he said nothing. Luna had shown the proper etiquette by serving the boss first, but it was clear that Gino didn't appreciate coming in second in his own home.

With a nervous glance at me and Enzo, she retreated from the room, forgetting to close the door this time.

My gaze followed her until she rounded the corner, then remained on the empty hall where I'd last seen her for a long moment before I did another sweep of the room and the other doorway that led into the rest of the house.

Had she liked the chicken I'd left her last night? Or did she enjoy the eggs more? I'd learned to cook on my own when I found that other people's cooking never seemed to measure up to my expectations, although Lisa—Luca's cook and housekeeper—did a fairly good job. I'd taught myself after...

Well, after I was free.

My mind wandered back to Luna as Gino regaled Luca with the story of the wine he'd had his chef choose for their meal. At the wedding, she'd been drinking a lemon drop martini. Did she like wine, or did she prefer sugary cocktails? What were her favorite foods? Favorite colors? Did she have any allergies? I needed to know everything about her. Where she'd come from and how she'd ended up in the foster system. What her childhood had been like. Who had given her her first kiss. Why she'd bet her life away to a man like Gino and let him use her body.

Did she, like many women who'd ended up where she is, do it because she believed it was her only choice? As Luca said? Either way, I didn't judge her for those choices. I was only curious. I wanted to know what made her tick.

But what I really wanted to fucking know was why, out of all the beautiful women in the world, this one had me by the balls.

No. That wasn't right. I wasn't interested in any kind of relationship with her. She was nothing but a temporary fascination. Probably brought on by my exposure to Luca and Enzo and their recent relationships. I wasn't jealous. I didn't wish to deprive them of that joy in their lives. But I didn't understand it. And maybe my fascination with Luna was just that—my way of trying to understand it. And once I did, she would no longer be a distraction and I could go back to my normal life.

As Luca and Gino droned on and on about Gino's position in the family and how he was ready to take on more responsibility, noticeably steering Luca away from the topic of the Irish, I kept my eyes on the doorway, watching for Luna. Except for that first time, she didn't look at me when she came back into the room to refill their wine glasses. That was probably smart, if the way Gino also watched her was any indication. Still, he caught me staring at her more than once, narrowing his eyes at me each time, but I wasn't threatened by him. Though I did want to ask him what he thought to accomplish by starving her. I knew from experience that if he beat her down enough, eventually, she would break.

I thought of the light behind her blue eyes dimming to nothing more than a dull reflection, and a red haze clouded my vision. My eyes once again found the empty doorway she'd disappeared through, and I fought to keep myself from striding through it, finding her, and dragging her out of this house.

I was still struggling to regulate my breathing when she returned and helped the chef serve the lunch. Drinking her in, I reminded myself of the reasons I couldn't throw her over my shoulder and walk away, namely because I wouldn't make it past the front door.

Enzo leaned toward me and asked quietly, "Are you alright?"

"I'm good."

After a moment, he straightened again.

Once she'd set everything on the table, I stepped forward to taste Luca's food before he consumed any of it, earning a glare from Gino.

"Eh, what is this, Luca? Do you really think I would poison your food like a woman?"

"Of course not," Luca placated him. "It's just a precaution, my friend. I have many more enemies these days, and all it takes is one snake to slither into your home." Though there was no accusation behind his words, it was clear that Luca found Gino's security measures were severely lacking, therefore making him a weak link within the family.

The barb hit its mark. "No one would dare," Gino said, his voice hard.

Luca gave him a tight smile, but said nothing more. He knew as well as I did that Gino's lack of security and egotistical power trip was just asking for trouble. And eventually, it would find him. We could only hope that when it did, it didn't ricochet throughout the entire family.

"The food is fine," I told Luca. He'd argued with me when I told him that one of us should start doing this, and with Enzo newly married, it should be me. I owed Luca everything. I wasn't going to take any risks with his life. And I didn't trust Gino. He'd been after the boss position since Luca's father, Luigi, was still alive. I wouldn't put it past him to use any methods available to take out the competition. Even something as cowardly as poison.

Luca thanked me and picked up a clean fork, moaning with pleasure when he stuck a piece of *bistecca fiorentina* in his mouth, the steak perfectly rare. "Mmm. Your chef has outdone herself this time, Gino."

Somewhat placated, Gino told him, "Don't be getting any ideas. I have no plans to give her up." The two men laughed, then got back to matters at hand, Gino forgetting the perceived insult as quickly as it had happened.

Luna only appeared one more time to refill their wine glasses with a new bottle, which Gino ordered her to leave on the table, and then he dismissed her back to her room. She hesitated, her blue eyes taking on a wild look until Gino noticed her still standing there and glared at her, his meaning clear to all in the room. Without a word, she spun around and rushed out.

"What's the situation with the Irish, Gino?" Luca's question broke through the tension in the room as he cut off another piece of meat. "Is this something I need to take care of?" Whether he spoke of the Irish or Gino's son, Salvatore, was hard to tell.

Gino kept eating. "I have it handled."

"Are you sure about that?"

"I am. I took Finn and Cian to dinner last night, and we came to an understanding."

"What understanding?"

Gino didn't answer.

"Gino, what deal did you make with the Irish?"

With a great sigh, he set down his fork, picked up his napkin, and dabbed at the corners of his mouth. "I offered them a twenty-five percent cut from the proceeds of our next delivery."

Luca stilled. "You did *what*?"

Throwing his hands in the air and shaking his head, Gino said, "It was that, or give them my son. What else would you have me do, Luca?" He didn't wait for an answer. "He's *mio figlio*. My *son*. I'm not giving him up to those fucking Irish over a drunken misunderstanding."

"Jesus fucking Christ, Gino."

"No one was even killed!" His voice rose. "They want me to hand over my boy so they can beat him to death, and I won't do it." He made a sound of disgust. "Why the fuck did they have to come here? They should've stayed in Seattle."

Pushing his plate to the side and laying his napkin on the table, Luca leaned forward. "Listen to me. I'm not giving up twenty-five percent of my drug money. Not to the Irish or anyone else. And you don't have the authority to make that kind of deal. I don't give a fuck what the situation is." He pointed at Gino's chest. "You fucking deal with this. Salvatore is not an innocent boy. He's a grown man. A dangerous man. If the Irish want him, give him to them. He can take care of himself. Or you work out something else. Something that does *not* involve me. I'm not giving them my money, and I'm not getting dragged into a fucking war because of your *stupid famiglia*."

Gino visibly bristled at the insult, but said nothing.

"I think we're done here." Luca pushed back his chair, and Enzo and I moved into position to escort him out.

Stopping behind Gino's chair, Luca leaned down to speak into his ear. "Do not push me, Gino. And do not overstep your bounds like this again. This is your only warning. *Comprendere?*" Without waiting for an answer, Luca straightened, buttoned his jacket, and pulled the cuffs of his dress shirt out from under the sleeves.

"*Compredere?*" he repeated.

"Yes, I understand," Gino answered. "I understand you're not fit to be head of this family. You don't even understand the meaning of the word."

"I understand perfectly well what a family is and my responsibilities to them. But your son's temper is your problem, not mine. Not any of the other capos. So *deal with it.*"

As we went to take our leave, three of Gino's men appeared, blocking the exits.

My hand went to the pistol under my jacket, as did Enzo's, his face hard beneath his sunglasses.

A cold smile teased the corners of Luca's mouth. "Are we doing this, then?"

A heartbeat passed. Then another, as we waited for Gino's decision. I shifted my weight, ready to jump in front of Luca as soon as the need arose.

But Gino lifted his hand and waved his men aside. "We are not."

Luca caught his gaze and held it for a long moment, then continued walking. Enzo and I followed, our hands still on our guns. When we reached the hall, I stopped and turned, facing Gino and his men while Enzo got Luca safely out of the house and into the SUV. A few seconds later, my cell phone vibrated in my pocket—Enzo letting me know it was good to leave—and I backed toward the door.

A movement to my right made me whip my head around in that direction. Luna stood in the kitchen doorway, watching me. Her eyes pleaded with me for a second, then she turned and rushed toward her room.

I gave no indication that I'd seen her, just continued to back away, knowing Enzo would cover my back from outside so no one snuck up on me. I made it to the SUV and climbed in the back with Luca. "I don't trust him," I told Luca as we pulled out of his driveway. "We need to do something about him before he gets too ballsy."

Luca said nothing. He didn't need to. I was only voicing what we all already knew.

We were a few minutes from the lake house when he broke the silence. "The Irishman who has a problem with Salvatore needs to be dealt with. An accident. Something that won't be tied to Gino or to me. Because he's not going to give them his son. Not even for the good of the family."

"Of course not," Enzo said. "I wouldn't either. But I can see why he did what he did. Family is important."

"No. I can't blame him for that. But we really can't afford a war with the Irish," Luca mused, almost to himself. "And handing over money to them makes me look weak, which is exactly why Gino made them that offer. So, instead, we need to make the problem go away. The Irish won't be able to prove anything, but the message will be received loud and clear by both parties. Salvatore can't have a problem with a dead man, and Gino will have no reason to try to sell me out."

"I can take care of it," I told him. "I'll do it tonight."

"I'll go with you," Enzo offered.

I appreciated the offer, but that wasn't going to work for me. I planned to sneak back to Gino's when I was finished. "That's not necessary. It'll be better if I go alone."

Luca thought about my offer for a minute, and as we pulled up to the front of the house, he finally gave his consent. "Make it clean," he told me. "None of your bullshit tonight, Tris. Get in and get out. No prints. No blood. Unless it's from him falling and hitting his head. In and out," he repeated.

"Of course," I promised, because I knew it was what he wanted to hear. Enzo met my eyes in the rearview mirror, but he said nothing. And I knew he wouldn't. I never did anything that would endanger anyone in this house. And I never would.

Even if sometimes I liked to play.

CHAPTER 8

Luna

I shivered as I remembered the dark eyes that met mine briefly in the hall before I ran back to my room. Cold, emotionless, and deadly, they'd reminded me of a snake about to strike.

As I'd stood there, frozen, hypnotized by Tristan's stare, my life flashed before of my eyes. Well, maybe not my entire life, but Logan's face sure did. I seriously expected this guy to put a bullet through my skull at any moment.

Then he'd blinked, breaking the spell, and the predator became more curious than hungry. I tried to silently plead with him not to say anything about seeing me there —since I was disobeying Gino's order to go directly to my room—but I had no idea if I'd gotten through to him or if he even cared. Why would he? So I'd taken a deep breath and rushed away, waiting for that slug to hit me in the back. But it never came.

Another shiver ran through me as I stared at the closed bedroom door without really seeing it.

Waiting.

Whether he'd understood what I was trying to say to him or not, he must not have said anything because no one came to my room to beat me for my insubordination. When Gino gave an order, he expected it to be followed immediately and without argument. No dilly-dallying. And definitely no trying to steal food like I had done.

Still, the sun was setting by the time I was able to relax enough to risk calling Logan.

Pulling my cell phone from the drawer in my nightstand, I curled up against the headboard of my bed and called my little brother to distract myself from how hungry I was already. All I'd had for lunch were the few bites I'd managed to swipe while the chef's back was turned.

He answered on the first ring. "Hey, Luni. What's up?"

I smiled when I heard his voice. So deep now, like a grown man. "Hey, little brother. How's school going?"

As always, his answer was short and sweet. "Good. My pharmacology professor is an ass, but other than that, I can't complain."

Logan was getting his Bachelor of Science Degree in Nursing, beating over seventy percent of applicants to get into the program. He was good with people, and he was gonna be a great nurse. Patients of all ages will be grateful to have him. Besides the fact that he's smart, tall, handsome, keeps himself in shape, and has a killer smile that makes all the girls swoon, he'd also been volunteering at hospitals and nursing homes since he was in high school.

I'd asked him once why he loved being around sick people so much, and he'd just shrugged and mumbled something about it being as good a career as any other. But I knew my brother, and I knew he hadn't picked this path for his life on a whim. He never did anything impulsively. Maybe someday he'd open up to me about it, but I wasn't going to push him. He'd tell me when he was good and ready, and not before. "Can you switch classes? Get a new professor?"

"Nah. I don't wanna go through all that. He's an ass, but he's pretty fair with our grades. And the devil you know and all that shit." I could relate to him there. "How're things with you? You're not working today?"

"Not till later," I lied. Logan knew I worked at the strip club. He just thought I was a server, not a dancer. I didn't know how much longer I'd be able to hide the fact that I no longer worked there though, now that he was twenty-two and could waltz into the club whenever the hell he wanted to. Lucky for me, he usually had better things to do with his time. He had no idea what I did, or what I'd done in the past, to keep a roof over our heads and food on the table. And that was okay. If he did, he'd feel guilty and probably quit school and start working some bullshit job so he could contribute more. But I hadn't sacrificed so much...so *fucking* much...just for him to mess up his life.

And, if I were honest, doing what I did didn't really bother me. Not anymore. I'd lost any feelings of shame or disgust a long time ago. And it was a quick way to make money and give us some security. But I knew if Logan found out, he'd lose his shit.

We chatted some more about his classes and then he told me he had to go get his homework done. "Okay," I told him. "I'll call you soon."

"Hey," he said before I could hang up. "You wanna have lunch tomorrow? I've got a long break between classes because one of my teachers is gonna be out, and she just gave us an assignment to do on our own time."

"Um..." I knew I couldn't. Gino would never allow it. Especially not now when he was being so damn moody. "I can't tomorrow. But...soon. Okay?"

He was quiet for a moment. "What's going on, Luni?"

"Nothing."

"You're lying to me. And I don't know why because you're a shit liar."

I had to smile, because I thought I was a pretty good liar. He just knew me too well. "Everything's fine, hon. I promise."

"Luni..."

"I promise," I repeated.

He sighed loudly. Along with knowing when I was lying, he also knew when he was wasting his energy with me, just like I did with him. I wasn't going to tell him anything, and he knew it. "Alright, well, if you can't have lunch tomorrow, then at least call me," he ordered. "It'll help pass the time."

"I'll try." It was the best I could give him.

"Alright. Love you."

"Love you back."

I hung up the phone and stared down at the screen for a long time. Then I burst into tears. Again. God, I was so sick and tired of feeling sorry for myself. But I couldn't help it. Every damn bad decision I'd made over the last few weeks was coming back to haunt me like a fucking poltergeist. But mostly I cried because I missed my little brother. And because I needed to figure out a way to explain to him why I wasn't living at home anymore before he went on break for the summer and came home to our apartment.

I cried for a long time. Until the ghosts of my past were exorcised, and there were no more tears left to shed.

Through blurry eyes, I looked over at the window. I could leave. I could just sneak out that window and run away and never look back. I could call Logan back and have him meet me somewhere and we could just...run.

It was a nice thought, and for a few minutes, I lost myself in the daydream.

But I knew without a doubt Gino would hunt me down. Not because he cared about me, but because I was a possession. Just like this house, or that ugly Renaissance Jesus painting hanging in the living room above the fireplace. He owned me. And he'd be pissed if I cheated him out of his winnings. Hell, he even paid for Logan.

No, he wouldn't let me go. If I ran and he let me get away with it, it would make him look like a laughingstock in front of his cronies. And the one thing Gino had in excess was pride. I had a feeling he'd been bullied too much in school or something, and now he spent his life proving to everyone that he wasn't weak. It was why he had such a hard time bowing down to anyone, even the boss of the Italian mafia.

I wiped the last of my tears from my cheeks. I'd overheard the end of his lunch with Luca. That man wasn't stupid, and Gino was a fool if he ever thought he would get one over on him. Plus, those two guards of his would never allow anyone to get anywhere near the boss. And they were some scary motherfuckers, even I could see that. Whatever Luca had done to earn their loyalty, it was unbreakable. As long as they were alive, Luca would be also.

My thoughts looped back around to Tristan. He hadn't spoken to me today, but I vividly remembered his voice from the day I'd met him at the wedding. It was low, quiet, slightly husky, utterly terrifying, and had sent shivers down my spine. It took me a few seconds to realize why. And then I figured it out.

It was because, like his eyes, his voice completely lacked emotion. There wasn't an ounce of warmth or coldness. No happiness. No sadness. No anger. No confusion. There was just...nothing.

How was I supposed to reach a man who felt nothing?

I frowned at my own impulsive thoughts. Where the hell had that come from? Maybe because he was the only other person I'd had any real contact with other than Gino's chef. I sniffed and chewed on my thumbnail as I thought about our encounter at the wedding, staring at the wall with swollen eyes. As cold as he seemed, he hadn't been entirely uninterested in me, if the way those black eyes had been glued to my face and body had been any indication. And, he *had* spoken to me, at least. Which was more than I could say for any of the other guards who'd been tasked with watching me. But what the hell did I think? That I could somehow seduce this guy, and he'd come riding up on his white horse to save me?

I laughed out loud, and it was an ugly sound. No one was going to save me. I'd known that since I was a kid. This was a man's world. And if I wanted to survive, I had to learn to play by their rules.

And whatever kind soul was bringing food for me, I would bet money it wasn't one of these mafia guys. None of Gino's associates gave a flying fuck about me or what he did to me. I was only a woman, after all. I wasn't dangerous. I wasn't a threat. And if I happened to get out of line, I had no doubt that any one of them would remove me from the situation without blinking. None of these guys were the knight in shining armor type.

Especially not a man with soulless eyes.

CHAPTER 9

Tristan

I found the Irishman I was looking for in one of the clubs where they usually hung out, the same club where Salvatore had tried to shoot him in the head. Just to be sure, I pulled a pair of binoculars from the glove box of the old, beat up Chevy I'd borrowed, then glanced down at the picture Luca texted me and compared this *stronzo's* neck tat to the one in the photo—a shamrock with the year 1992 along the stem. Not very original, but it was enough to confirm I had the right guy.

Parked down the street out of range of the cameras, I watched him walk inside. He was alone. Hopefully, he would leave the same way after consuming half his body weight in some good Irish whiskey. It would make my job easier. And I was impatient to get it done and see Luna.

A few hours later, the bouncer helped him out and put him in an Uber. I smiled, started the car, and followed them to the other side of the city where the Irishman lived in a high-rise condo near the capitol building.

Perfect.

Swinging into a guest spot, I parked, pulled a baseball cap over my eyes, and met the Irishman and his driver as he was helping him to the front door.

"Why the hell do you do this to yourself, man?" I asked as I reached for him. "It's okay," I told the driver. "I can take him from here."

"You know this guy?" he asked. But by the way he was happily handing him off to me, I knew it wouldn't really matter what my answer was.

"Yeah," I told him. "He's my neighbor. I'll get him upstairs."

"Cool. Thanks." Without a second glance, he let him go and walked back to his car.

Inside, I dragged the Irishman to the front desk. "Hey, Tony."

"Hey." Never taking his eyes off the monitor, my associate I'd called earlier tapped away at the keyboard.

"Any problems getting in here tonight?"

"Nope."

"Good." I didn't ask where the real concierge was or what he'd done with them. I didn't care. As I waited, I awkwardly pulled on a pair of gloves without dropping my "neighbor" on the floor. The guy was pretty much out of it, which would be a blessing for him. He wouldn't see what's coming.

A few seconds later, Tony hit enter and nodded. "You're good. We just had a glitch with the cameras. You've got eight minutes until they come back online."

"Perfect." Rummaging around in the Irishman's pockets, I found his keys. "What's his condo number?"

Tony found the number, and I half carried, half walked the Irishman to the elevator.

Four minutes later, I watched as he accidentally took his own life by falling over the balcony. His skull exploded upon impact. I left the patio door open, tossed his keys on the coffee table, and locked the door to his condo, pulling it closed behind me. When I reached the lobby, a woman was screaming and crying at Tony for him to call an ambulance.

Outside, I walked around the block until I was directly beneath the Irishman's balcony. The body was there, broken and bloody, one leg twisted at a strange angle. Even with the early morning hour, I was slightly surprised there wasn't a crowd gathering. Keeping my face shielded by the cap in case anyone was watching, I knelt by the body and rearranged his leg so it looked normal.

"Godspeed to hell," I told him as I took off my gloves and ran my fingers through the blood spreading out beneath his head. "I'll see you when I get there." For we would all end up there in the afterlife. I had no doubt.

I heard the distant wail of sirens as I walked back to the car.

It was after three in the morning by the time I made it back to Gino's. The entire house was dark and quiet, with only the three guards from earlier watching the perimeter.

I edged closer to Luna's window. By the light of the partial moon, I could barely make out a lump on the bed where she slept curled up under the comforter. Slow and easy, I removed the screen and eased the window up a few inches.

She didn't move.

Opening it the rest of the way, I crawled through the opening into her room, bringing a rush of cold air with me. I looked around for the container of food I'd left for her the night before so I could remove the evidence, but I didn't see it. I hoped she'd hidden it somewhere and that it hadn't been found.

As I set the screen back in place without fastening it and shut the window in case one of the guards happened to wander by, I wondered if she'd managed to talk the chef into giving her some of the lunch she'd helped with. I hadn't had time to make her anything tonight, but I would make it up to her tomorrow.

Quietly, I walked over to the bed. Luna slept on her side, hugging the extra pillow. The skin around her eyes was red and puffy, as though she'd been crying. The sight tugged on something in the middle of my chest. Something I didn't recognize. I frowned as I tried to identify what it was, but eventually, my attention was drawn back to Luna.

Earbuds were in her ears, and I found myself curious to know what she was listening to. A cell phone was on the nightstand. I tapped the screen and a Spotify list popped up with the sounds of a rainstorm playing, set on repeat. I was surprised Gino allowed her to have a phone.

Holding it to her sleeping face to unlock it, I opened the home screen and scrolled through her calls and messages. The last call was to someone named Logan. Her brother. All her texts were to him also. Didn't she have any friends? It would be better if she didn't. It would make things easier if no one would be looking for her.

It didn't occur to me to wonder why I'd had that thought.

Closing out that screen, I tapped the icon for her info page and entered her number into my phone. Then I scrolled through some of her photos. Most were of her and her brother. I recognized him from the image Luca had shown me on his computer. There were also several photos of Austin landmarks. The Stevie Ray Vaughan statue by Lady Bird Lake, along with the guitar statues located on random sidewalks downtown, the view of the capitol building on Congress Ave, and a bunch of candid shots of the homeless sleeping in doorways and along the hike and bike trail.

I wondered what her fascination was with those people. Was it empathy that drove her to take these photos? Or fear of becoming one of them?

Sending the selfies of her that I liked to myself, I swiped around a little more, but saw nothing else of interest, so I set her phone back on her nightstand.

In the glow of the screen, I noticed blood on the back of my hand near my wrist and wiped it on my pants.

Luna continued to sleep, her lips parted and her breath coming in soft snores. I watched her for a while, wondering what she was dreaming about and wishing I could penetrate her mind to see for myself. Her hair was pulled back in a long braid, except for a few wayward strands that had pulled loose and fallen over her forehead. Without thinking, I reached toward her to carefully brush it away from her eyes. My hand shook when I realized what I was doing, and I paused with my fingers barely an inch from touching her. Then I took a deep breath and carefully brushed the strands away from her eyes. I waited for the sick twist in my stomach I always felt when I touched someone, but there was... nothing.

I rubbed the strands between my fingertips. They were soft. So soft. And black as my soul in the darkness. Bending over her prone body, I lifted them to my nose. Her hair smelled freshly washed, with a light, clean fragrance that made me want to undo her braid and gather it all up in large handfuls so I could bury my face in the scent and breathe her in.

When I realized what I was doing, I stiffened. What the hell was she doing to me?

With a sense of something akin to wonder, I bent closer and watched as I let the strands sift through my fingers to settle back against her head. This close, her warm skin smelled delicious. I wanted to run my tongue along her jaw and taste it. Skimming the tip of my nose over the soft skin that covered the side of her throat, I inhaled the scent into my lungs. A low growl rumbled deep within my chest, and I forced myself to straighten before I woke her.

I felt strangely unsettled, my breath fast and erratic, my skin raw and overly sensitive. Blood raced through my veins as I watched her sleep, confused, and yet unable to tear my eyes away. Stumbling backward, I fought to break the bizarre connection tethering me to her, but she held me captive without even trying. I wanted to scoop her up into my arms and take her away from here. Take her home.

But that was crazy.

It was suddenly too much. Desperate to return to my senses, I slammed the palm of my hand against the fastening of my pants, pressing the zipper painfully into my swollen cock. The pain didn't make me any less hard, but it did distract me enough that I was able to tear my eyes away from her beautiful face.

Not yet ready to leave, I let my curiosity take me across the room and into the bathroom, the one room of hers I hadn't been in yet. Closing the door behind me so I didn't wake her, I turned on the light. Beige walls nearly blended into the marbled countertop, which had veins of the same color throughout its creamy surface. Numerous plastic bottles littered its surface. I picked up the first one—a lotion—and brought it to my nose. It smelled like Luna's skin, and my cock reacted violently. I allowed myself to indulge for a few more seconds before I turned my face away. Setting it down, I checked out her toothbrush, toothpaste, and mouthwash, noting the brands she used. A glass bottle was tucked in the corner. The label read "Dioriviera." I unscrewed the top and smelled it, wincing and quickly capping it again. I recognized the fruity, floral scent from the day I'd met her. I didn't like it any more now than I did then. But it was more than that. Something that knocked on the back door of my memories but wouldn't come through.

I put the bottle in my pocket to dispose of later. I would replace it with something more pleasant the next time I came.

Lifting my eyes to the mirror, I caught my reflection, and the sight made me frown. Blood was smeared across my cheek and hands, and I could see the shiny wetness of it on the black material of my sleeves and the front of my pants. My eyes shifted to the right, where I could see her shower in the reflection over my shoulder. I imagined her in there, water running over her pale soapy skin, dripping from her hardened nipples, and my pulse picked up before I was once again distracted by my appearance.

I cocked my head. I didn't want her to wake up and see me covered in blood. For one, it would most likely frighten her. And second, she didn't need to know what she didn't need to know. There was nothing I could do about my clothes, but if the lights were off, maybe she wouldn't notice if she did happen to wake. My skin, however, was lighter. Therefore, it would be much more noticeable.

I glanced at the bathroom door. All was quiet in the room beyond it. This idea probably wasn't the smartest one I'd ever had. I should just leave and come back again when I wasn't covered in the evidence of my crimes. But the temptation to wash myself in the same place she did was too much to resist.

Unfastening my shoulder holster, I removed it and laid both it and my gun where it would be within easy reach.

Next, I unlaced my boots and took them off. My socks followed. Then I pulled my shirt over my head and folded it so the blood spatters were on the inside before I dropped it to the floor, careful to keep it on the tiles where I could easily wipe up any blood that happened to get on them. I unfastened my pants, shoved them off, and laid them on my shirt, along with my boxer briefs.

My cock pulsed in anticipation as I opened the glass door and started the water. As I waited for it to heat up, I opened the cabinet underneath the sink. There was only a box of tampons and a hair dryer. I closed it again, then I checked the temperature of the water in the shower and stepped inside. I didn't bother to lock the bathroom door, a part of me wishing Luna would wake up and find me here. Although I wondered how she'd react if she did. Would she scream? Would she watch? Or would she join me?

I'd never know if I locked the door.

The spray from the large, round shower head sluiced over me like a waterfall. I let it wash away my sins, tilting my head back to wet my hair and running my hands over my face to remove what I could with water alone. Then I found her shampoo and pumped some of it into my palm. My eyes closed as I lathered up my hair, as close to bliss as I've ever been for as long as I could remember. The scent of her hair filled the small space, enhanced by the warm water. I breathed it into my aching lungs as I leaned my head back under the spray of water and let it wash the suds out of my hair and down my body, reveling in the feel of them as they traveled down my bare chest and back, then over my ass and groin. My hands followed the bubbles down my slick stomach, feeling the familiar bumps and ridges of the scars that covered me. I rubbed the scent into my skin, down to my cock, which jutted out from my hips. It was fully engorged, harder than I'd ever seen it.

I gripped myself in my palm with a hiss. It felt so fucking good I had to brace my other hand on the shower wall so my legs wouldn't collapse beneath me. The warm water caressed my back as I ran my fist up and down my length with slow, languid strokes. Closing my eyes, I imagined Luna on her knees in front of me, her hands tied behind her back and her perfect mouth stretched around my dick. Her blue eyes were on mine, and her soft hair was gripped in my hands as she sucked me down her throat.

Could I handle her lips on me? The feel of her warm, wet mouth and soft tongue?

In real life? I had no fucking idea. But in my fantasy, it was the best fucking thing I'd ever felt in my life.

My fist tightened around my cock as my entire body tensed. I didn't want to rush this, but fucking hell, this was the sweetest torture I'd ever experienced. And I'd had more than my fair share. My muscles screamed as I stroked faster, harder, my breathing harsh and my hips thrusting forward to meet my hand, imagining now it was Luna's sweet pussy clenched around me. And I knew it would be sweet. Just like the rest of her. I wanted to taste her. Wanted to feel her mouth on me in return. Feel her hands. The weight of her body.

As the thought of her freely touching me entered my fantasy out of nowhere, ice-cold fear slithered down my spine, locking my muscles and chasing away the pleasure. Moisture that had nothing to do with the shower filled my eyes. With a low growl, I shook away reality, reminding myself this was just a fantasy. Instead, I concentrated on the orgasm tightening my balls and sliding down my cock. It slammed into me so hard I turned my head and bit into my bicep to muffle the sounds erupting from my chest. The copper taste of blood coated my tongue as spurts of white cum shot from the head of my cock, painting the shower wall in front of me and dribbling down my hand. It was the longest orgasm I'd ever had, going on and on until my knees shook and I could barely hold myself upright.

Easier now, I stroked myself a few more times, then gently removed my hand and opened my eyes.

My entire body shuddered, and for a moment, all I could do was stand there in awe, wrapped in the images of us together, until something dark and lonely washed over me, so harsh it nearly sent me to my knees for real this time.

I wasn't in the fantasy with Luna.

I was alone.

Always alone.

Gritting my teeth, I watched the evidence of my desecration run down the tiles. With my hand, I spread it around until it blended in and wouldn't be noticed. The next time Luna showered, it would be in my cum.

I found the soap and finished washing myself, making sure all the blood went down the drain before I shut off the water.

By the time I dried myself off with her towel, whatever the hell had happened to me in the shower had settled somewhat. I hung her towel back where I'd found it and put my clothes and boots back on. Most of the blood had dried and wasn't so noticeable now. Picking up her brush, I ran it through my hair, brushing back the longer strands on top away from my face before I put on my shoulder holster.

With a quick look around to make sure I hadn't left anything, I turned off the light and quietly opened the door. Luna had rolled over and was now sleeping on her other side, and I could see the bare skin of one shoulder where the sheet had ridden down, covered only by the thin strap of some type of tank top. Her earbuds were still in her ears.

I crept over to the bed and stared at that stretch of pale skin. So smooth and unmarked. Like her hair, I wanted to feel the texture so badly that I instinctively reached toward her. I got so close I felt the warmth radiating from her skin before I managed to come to my senses and stopped with the tips of my fingers less than half an inch from her shoulder. Curling my hand into a fist, I pulled my arm back.

Luna was not mine to touch. And she never would be. No woman would ever be mine.

That all too familiar feeling of being alone in the darkness descended over me, and my insides hollowed out. I needed to leave before I did something stupid. Like climb into bed with her.

Checking that my phone, the strands of her hair, and that horrible bottle of perfume were still in my pockets, I went out the way I'd come in, closing the window and fastening the screen back into place. Then I jogged back to the SUV, not bothering to watch for Gino's men, who were probably dozing on the front entryway where they'd been when I'd come in. At least, I hoped they were. If either of them showed themselves, they wouldn't be waking up tomorrow.

And I didn't want anything interfering with my visits to see Luna.

CHAPTER 10

Luna

When I woke up, my eyes were still swollen from my self-pity party the night before, so I took a quick shower and pressed a cold, wet washcloth to my eyes. It helped reduce the swelling a bit, and after a few minutes, I felt a little more human.

I pulled on a long-sleeved green shirt that I knew Gino liked. The tight cotton accentuated my breasts and flared out over my hips, but was short enough that it didn't hide my ass in the washed-out jeans I wore with it. I didn't bother with shoes, just some thick socks because the house felt cold this morning.

Testing my bedroom door, I found it was unlocked. I pulled it open and glanced up and down the hall. I didn't see anyone, but I heard voices coming from the direction of the kitchen, and the strong aroma of bacon teased my nose. My stomach rumbled loudly. Following the smell of food, I made my way to the dining room.

As I approached the doorway, I heard Gino talking to someone and hesitated. I almost turned around and went back to my room, but my growling stomach convinced me to at least peek inside.

Gino spotted me right away. "Luna. Come get some breakfast."

He waved me in, and I headed to the breakfast buffet set up along the sidewall as Gino's attention returned to the man sitting with him. I quickly glanced at the back of his head, but I didn't recognize him. However, that didn't mean much. Gino was always talking to people. I honestly didn't pay much attention to what he was doing or with who unless it directly affected me. Otherwise, it was none of my business.

I made myself a plate, planning to take it back to my room so I didn't interrupt them, when he surprised me by saying, "Luna, why don't you bring over the pot of coffee with you."

Recognizing a demand when I heard one, I grabbed the coffeepot, balancing my orange juice in the crook of my arm as I took it, my plate, and the coffee to the table. I set it down in front of him with a small smile, then stood awkwardly with my plate while he refilled his cup.

"Join us," he told me. "Luna, this is Milo. Milo, this is my...companion, Luna."

The man sitting with Gino was younger than I'd expected, with bright, mossy green eyes that were startling in their intensity. A mustache covered his upper lip, attached to a short beard that was little more than a five o'clock shadow, and did nothing to hide his angular jaw. His shaggy, blond hair reminded me of a surfer, and the defined muscles of his shoulders and arms were noticeable even underneath his long-sleeved, navy blue shirt. A black hoop earring adorned his left ear. His shy smile and boy next door looks didn't fool me, though. Anyone associated with Gino was dangerous in one way or another. "Nice to meet you," I told him with a small smile as I sat down with my plate.

"Same," he said. Without taking his eyes off me, he asked Gino, "Where the hell did you get a looker like this one?"

Gino glanced up from his plate where he was scraping up the last of his egg yolk with a slice of toast. "I won her in a poker game."

Milo's eyebrows shot up. "No shit? Who the hell would be stupid enough to bet a treasure like this?"

"Me," I told him as I cut into my pancakes. "I did."

Gino laughed. "Gave me a run for my money, she did. It was pure luck that I ended up with the hand I had."

"Luck? Or cheating?" Milo asked him with a grin.

Gino set down his coffee mug a little harder than necessary. "Are you calling me a cheater, boy?"

My fork stilled on its way back to my plate, and my muscles tensed, prepared to jump up and dive under the table if shots suddenly broke out. But I was taking my damn breakfast with me.

But Milo just smiled harder. "Nah. I'm not saying that at all. But hell, Gino. I'd cheat my ass off to get a hold of a girl like this."

The tension filling the room left as fast as it had come on. "Eh. You get your eyes off her, boy. Luna isn't for sale." Then he chuckled, pleased that another man coveted what was his.

Milo winked at me.

Winked.

I fought the smile threatening to break across my face. He was totally fucking with Gino. The guy had balls, I had to give him that. It didn't make me relax around him, but it made breakfast a hell of a lot more amusing.

"So," Gino said, interrupting our silent mirth. "You sure you have nothing on Luca or his two apes that you can give to me? Nothing at all?"

Lowering my eyes, I continued eating my breakfast, but my ears were wide open this time.

"Afraid not," Milo told him. "And even if I did, I wouldn't tell you, Gino. That's why you guys keep me alive."

Just what exactly did this guy do for them? He wasn't mafia. I could tell that right away. And not just because he had blond hair, green eyes, and pale skin, unlike the darker complected Italians I was surrounded by in this house. I knew because of his mannerisms and the way he talked. He was respectful, but it wasn't ingrained in him like the mafia families. It was possible he was a made man, but I doubted it. Most likely, he was some type of mercenary, paid well to keep his mouth shut. So why Gino was trying to get information out of him was beyond me. Talking was a death sentence. Even I knew that.

"No, that's not the reason," Gino told him. "We keep you alive because you're the best at what you do."

"Thank you," he responded with a smile that sent gooseflesh skating across my arms.

"Luna, the coffee is gone. Get Milo another pot."

I shoved some scrambled eggs into my mouth, then set my fork down and reached across the table for the empty pot. "Of course. How do you like it?" I asked as I chewed. I was too hungry for manners.

"Just a little half and half, please."

Leaving the table, I retrieved the full coffeepot and the half and half and brought them back to the table. They'd both lowered their voices when I got up, and I couldn't make out what they were saying, but the conversation was heating up by the time I returned.

As I approached the table, Gino waved his hand in front of him and made a face like something in the room stunk. "Non me ne frega un cazzo!" he shouted. *I don't give a shit!*

I paused briefly before setting the coffeepot and creamer down near Milo. He thanked me as he poured another cup, but there was no smile this time.

As I walked back around to my seat, I glanced at Gino to see if he wanted me to leave now, but he completely ignored me. I hesitated again, then sat back down and went about finishing my breakfast. Being uncomfortable for a few minutes was far better than starving all day.

"I think we're done here, Gino." Milo took a sip of his coffee, set it back on the table, then scooted his chair back.

I braced for another show of Gino's temper, but he just shook his head and huffed out a laugh. "Sì, sì. We're done. There's no need to make Luna suffer through any more of this business talk. But sit, Milo. Sit! Let's enjoy our coffee and Luna's company, eh? It's a beautiful morning."

It was cold and rainy. A typical Texas winter day. But after a glance in my direction, Milo shrugged and pulled his chair back up to the table. His green eyes landed on me as he picked up his coffee cup. "So. Luna. What do you do with yourself? Besides bet your life away gambling, I mean."

I laughed. I couldn't help it. "Um, I'm a dancer at Honey's. At least, I was," I corrected myself. "Up until a few weeks ago. I'm on an extended leave of absence," I clarified. The owner of the club was present for our poker game, and assured me I'd still have a job if and when I was able to come back.

"Do you miss it?"

"Excuse me?"

"Dancing," he said. "Do you miss dancing? Or are you glad Gino stole you away from that life?"

I thought about it for a minute. "I don't miss it or not miss it," I told him. "It was a job."

Gino made a face. "Don't let her fool you. She misses dirty old men ogling her tits and ass."

"No," I told him. "I miss making fools of those dirty old men by taking all their money." I didn't mention the fact that he'd been one of those men for months before he won me. And I was still taking his money. I just had to give up a little more for it now.

They both laughed. Gino's was a little self-deprecating.

Milo cocked his head as he studied me. "You said you worked at Honey's?"

Unable to fit any more food into my stomach, I set down my fork and took a sip of my juice. "Mmhmm."

"Why are you looking at her like that?" Gino asked.

I lifted my eyes to find that Milo was indeed staring at me hard.

"I'm just trying to place where I know her from," he told Gino.

He waved away his question. "You've probably seen her dance."

"No, that's not it. I've never been in Honey's."

"Pfft," Gino scoffed. "A young boy like you? Never been in a strip bar?"

"I didn't say that," Milo answered. "I said I've never been in Honey's. But no, I don't usually blow my money on exotic dancers. I have plenty of women showing me their tits for free." He laughed, and Gino joined in, smacking him on the arm a few times.

My eyes went back and forth between them as they talked about me like I wasn't there. I would've left the table, but the only place to go was back to my room, and I wasn't quite ready to be stuck in there again. Besides, now that Gino was feeding me again and leaving my door unlocked, I didn't want to risk pissing him off by leaving the table before I was dismissed.

Milo caught me looking at him. "Have you always hung around with these guys?" he asked me directly. "Maybe I've seen you at a dinner or a party or something."

I knew exactly what he meant. He was wondering if I was one of the girls that got passed around between the capos. "Uh, no. Only at the club."

"Huh." He stared at me for a few more seconds, then shrugged. "I can't figure it out. But I will eventually." Tapping his temple with his forefinger, he smiled. "It'll come to me."

Why did that make me nervous? From the corner of my eye, I noticed Cino's chin raise and his jaw tightened. "Luna, why don't you excuse yourself and go back to your room?"

"Of course." I quickly rose from the table and picked up my plate and glass. "It was nice meeting you," I told Milo. "Please, excuse me."

He didn't respond, but I felt both men's eyes on me as I took my dirty dishes to the buffet table, where I left them in the empty bin and rushed from the room. Something weird was going on, and I was more than happy to remove myself from the growing tension.

I took my time going back to my room, wandering around the house a bit until I found myself in the informal living room that guests rarely saw. I stared at the couch in front of the large television, remembering a similar setup in a different place and the man who'd taken so many liberties with me on a piece of furniture very similar to this one. Invisible fingers crawled over my skin, eerily soft for a man, the memories way too real even after all these years.

I blinked, and the memory faded away, but not the feelings that came with it. I took a shaky breath, then forced them away. Nothing would come of reliving that time. It was over. In the past. And couldn't hurt me now.

Behind the couch stood a large bookshelf that held quite a number of books for a man who lost his patience if a text message was too long. Unable to imagine Gino ever reading anything more extensive than a menu, I looked over the titles, hoping to find something even remotely interesting to help me pass the time in my prison cell of a room.

I was on the third shelf when the hair on the back of my neck rose like someone was staring at me. Fear shot through me, and I spun around with the book I'd been looking at still in my hands, my mouth open to explain to Gino why I wasn't already back in my room.

But it wasn't Gino leaning against the doorway, it was one of his guards. The one with dull, heavy-lidded eyes, thick lips, and a receding hairline he didn't try to hide. Guido? Gary? Something like that.

"I was just grabbing a book," I explained quickly. Keeping the one I had and picking another one without even looking at the title, I tried to rush past him and head back to my room.

But he grabbed my upper arm, stopping me. "Not so fast, girl."

Squeezing my eyes shut, I barely resisted the urge to knee him in the groin.

"Let me see those books you're trying to steal."

I sighed. "I'm not stealing them. Where the hell would I take them? I'm just borrowing them so I'll have something to do."

"Does Gino know you're taking them?"

I pressed my lips together and didn't respond.

"Uh huh. So you're stealing them." From the corner of my eye, I watched him look up and down the hallway before pushing himself off the wall and forcing me back into the room, his fingertips digging hard into my flesh.

I tried to yank my arm from his grip. "Let me go. Before I scream this house down."

He ignored my threat. "I'll tell you what," he said once he'd gotten me out of the doorway and away from the eyes of anyone who might be in the hall. "I'll let you take the books if you pay me for them."

I almost laughed in his face. Did he think he was being clever? I knew this game, probably a hell of a lot better than he did, and I hadn't played it since I was eighteen. "I'm not stealing, I'm borrowing. And you know what?"

He lifted his eyebrows in question.

"I don't feel like reading anymore," I told him. Then I violently yanked my arm from his grip and marched over to the bookshelf, setting the books back on the shelf where I'd found them. Without so much as a glance in his direction, I stalked past him and out the door.

It wasn't until I was inside my room with the door closed behind me that I raised my shaking hands and covered my face, fighting back the tears that threatened.

CHAPTER 11

Luna

My eyes drifted open. It was still dark, and for a brief moment, I didn't know where I was. When I remembered, I moaned with disappointment. In the faint light of the nightlight I left on in the bathroom, I could barely see the lazy rotation of the ceiling fan. It didn't matter how cold it was outside, I couldn't sleep without the ceiling fan on.

As I watched it, the heaviness of sleep weighed down my eyelids again, and I breathed in deeply through my nose and tried to stretch, then roll over.

Two things hit me at the same time.

One was the smell. It wasn't an unpleasant smell. Just the opposite. It was dark and spicy and filled me with peace, even as it made my pulse pick up with interest. Like a waterfall in a fragrant forest.

Second was the fact that I couldn't move my arms or legs.

Alarm shot through me, and my eyes flew wide open as my brain—still half in the dream I'd been having—tried to catch up with this new reality. I tugged my right arm. Something bound my wrist. It didn't hurt, but it was tight enough that I couldn't slip my hand out. Same with my other wrist and both of my ankles.

I was on my back, tied spread eagle to my bed. The sheet and comforter were pushed down to my waist, my tied ankles still underneath them.

"Are you going to scream?"

The voice came out of the darkness to my left, and I whipped my head in that direction. My sleepy brain tried to place it as I searched for the body it was attached to. Something moved, and I vaguely made out the outline of a dark form not five feet from my bed. "What?" My voice was dry and husky with sleep.

"Are you going to scream?" he repeated. "Because if you are, I'll have to gag you. Or drug you. And I'd rather not do that."

"I'd rather you didn't do that, either," I answered honestly. If I was drugged, I couldn't fight back. "So no. I won't scream." Not yet, anyway.

"Good," he told me.

I felt his eyes on me, like an electric current zipping across my skin. Or maybe it was just my imagination. I waited for him to say more, and when he didn't, I asked the obvious question. "Why am I tied to the bed?"

"Because I don't want you to touch me."

My racing heart slowed down a notch. "If I promise I won't touch you, will you untie me?"

There was no answer.

"Hello?"

"No," he said.

"Where's Gino?"

I heard the soft rustle of clothing and saw the dark form move slightly as he shifted positions, as though my question made him uncomfortable. But his tone, when he responded, betrayed nothing. "In his bed, I would imagine."

"So he's still alive?"

"Yes. For now," he added. "He'll stay that way unless you make him come in here."

I wasn't sure whether to feel relieved or disappointed about that bit of news and hung somewhere between the two. "I won't do that."

There was another long silence, the only sound the heavy beat of my heart pounding in my ears. I breathed through it, trying to stay calm and control the panic rising inside of me.

My imagination raced through every horrible scenario of what could possibly happen from here. Why the hell was he just standing there staring at me? The anticipation was worse than anything he could do to me. My nerves were stretched so taut, I didn't know whether to laugh or cry. "What do you want?" I finally asked.

After a pause, he said quietly, "I don't know, exactly."

"How did you get in here?" I demanded.

Nothing.

I made the question more specific. "How did you get into my room?"

"Does it really matter?"

No, I guess it didn't. "Can you at least tell me who you are?"

"I apologize." His steps were silent as he moved closer to the bed and into the faint light shining in from the bathroom.

I'd only seen him twice before, and he was dressed differently this time—in black cargo pants and a long-sleeved black shirt with a high neckline instead of a suit—so it took me a second to realize who it was. "Tristan?"

Dark eyes, nearly hidden in shadows, traveled down my body before they found their way back up to my face. He didn't say anything, but I didn't miss the movement of his Adam's apple as he swallowed hard.

Shit. Shit. My blood chilled, and the next words flew from my mouth before I could stop them. "Are you going to hurt me?" My mind returned to the conversation I'd heard between Gino and Milo. Was he here to get back at Gino for something? Thinking if he did something to me, it would bring the mafia capo down?

But he shook his head slightly. "No."

Somehow, that didn't make me feel better. Before I could ask him anything else, he spoke.

"I wanted to talk to you."

"Talk?"

"Yes. Just talk."

"About what, exactly? Because I don't know anything. Gino doesn't tell me anything." I was babbling, but I couldn't help it. Despite his assurances, my nerves were still screaming.

"Not about Gino. About you."

"Me?"

"Yes."

He went quiet again, and I tugged on the restraints. "Would you please untie me?"

Another slight shake of his head was his only answer.

As I looked around the room for help that wasn't going to appear, I swallowed down the panic that was still threatening to rise, screaming, from my throat. "Tristan, please." I was quickly discovering I didn't like being restrained without my knowledge or permission. I'd never really gotten into BDSM or any kind of heavy kinks. I turned my pleading eyes back to the man beside my bed just in time to see him reaching a hand toward me.

So lightly I could barely feel them, the backs of his fingertips grazed my cheekbone and then my jaw, and I forgot all about the bonds holding me on the bed.

My voice was little more than a whisper. "What are you doing?"

His forehead furrowed in a mixture of confusion and concentration, his eyes following the trail of his fingers as they continued down the side of my throat and over my collarbone. There, they stilled. "So soft," he whispered. "I never knew it would be so soft."

My eyes flew to his face, and there was barely enough light for me to see his jaw clench.

"You said you wouldn't hurt me," I reminded him. My heart was racing so fast now I felt lightheaded. I fought the sensation, knowing I couldn't pass out. Not with this psychopath looking at me like he wanted to tear the skin from my body so he could pet it whenever he wanted to.

His eyes shifted from my body, locking onto mine. "Am I hurting you?" He didn't sound concerned, only curious, which sent another shiver down my spine.

"No," I answered honestly.

His attention dropped down to my breasts, covered only by the tank top I was wearing with my pajama shorts. "Your skin always looks so soft. Like your hair. I needed to see for myself."

He'd touched my hair? When I was sleeping? "I'd rather you didn't touch me. You don't have my permission to touch me." I wasn't sure if there was any decent part of this guy that I would reach this way, but I had to try.

"I won't hurt you."

"That doesn't matter. I don't want you to touch me, Tristan."

"I have to." The words were said so quietly I barely heard them over the sound of my own staggered breathing. "Don't scream," he ordered, slightly louder this time. "I won't hurt you," he repeated.

A knife appeared in his hand, and before I could even comprehend that he had a weapon and my life was about to end, cold metal kissed my breastbone. Keeping the dull edge against my skin, he slid the blade underneath my tank and between my breasts, slicing through the cotton of my tank. The knife disappeared, and he grabbed the two ragged edges of material and yanked, tearing my shirt all the way down to my stomach and exposing the inner curves of my breasts.

Tears gathered in my eyes, blurring my vision until I couldn't see. *Scream!* I told myself. *Scream, dammit!* But fear clamped around my throat like a vice, and nothing would come out.

His harsh intake of breath was loud in my ears, and then I felt his fingers skimming along my skin as he pushed the remains of my top to either side as far as he could, exposing my nipples. They hardened from the cold air, and I turned my face away and squeezed my eyes shut. There was nothing I could do to stop him at this point. I tried again to scream. I opened my mouth and everything. But nothing came out. I wasn't sure if it was fear for Gino or fear for myself that kept me from uttering a single sound, but I couldn't help but think that if Gino saw me like this, somehow it wouldn't matter that I was tied up and had no control over what was happening, he'd still find a way to blame me.

So I did what I did best and tried to go into my head. To another place and time where I wasn't being molested in my own bed.

And I succeeded.

Partially.

But a part of me—a small part, but a part nonetheless—was still fully aware that Tristan was staring down at me, devouring the sight of my body. Heat pooled between my thighs in a rush, an involuntary reaction of need I didn't understand. I'd never reacted this way to a man before.

I nearly jumped out of my skin when the tip of his finger skimmed the hard tip of my nipple, first one, and then the other. But what surprised me even more was the red-hot bolt of pure desire that shot from my nipples straight to my groin. My eyes flew open as I sucked in a breath, waiting to see what he would do next.

No. No. I didn't want this.

Closing my eyes again, I tried like hell to think of something else. Anything else.

"Don't do that," he gritted out.

I didn't know what he was talking about. I wasn't doing anything. I couldn't. I was tied to the fucking bed, desperately trying not to freak out. So I stayed silent.

"Luna. Look at me."

That deep, cold voice saying my name sent a shiver down my spine. But I did as he ordered. Maybe if I didn't piss him off, I'd have a chance of making it out of this alive and relatively unharmed.

Tentatively, I turned my head and opened my eyes. When they met his, he told me, "Don't do that again. I don't like it when you do that."

"Do what?" I whispered.

"Leave me," he said. "Don't do it again."

Confused, I could only stare up at him. "That would be kind of hard, what with me being tied up and all." I couldn't keep the sarcasm and frustration from my voice as I glared up at him, still terrified, but Jesus Christ, I wished he'd just get whatever he was planning the hell over with.

"I know what you're doing when you squeeze your eyes shut and turn away from me. It's the same thing you do when Gino is fucking you."

My heart stuttered in my chest. How did he know that? Had he been *watching* me? My mind went back to the night after the wedding when I'd noticed someone standing outside my window but hadn't been able to get a good look at him. The same night I'd first met Tristan.

Oh, my god. It wasn't one of Gino's guards. It was *him*.

His voice lowered. "But I'm not Gino. And I require you to be both physically *and* mentally present at all times when we're together. Do you understand?"

My cheeks burned. "Yes," I whispered.

"Good." His eyes dropped back down to my bare breasts. "I like looking at you. You're very beautiful. Do you know that?"

I couldn't respond because his hand was reaching for me once again. I held my breath as I waited for his touch, jumping slightly when it came, even though I'd been expecting it.

The calloused roughness of his fingertips skimmed light as a feather over the inner curve of my breast, then made a circle around my areola. I caught myself arching into his touch and froze, wondering what the hell was wrong with me. But if he'd noticed, he gave no indication.

A blast of cold air hit my bare legs as he ripped the covers off the lower half of my body, tossing them down to the bottom of the bed by my feet. I expected him to go right for the goods between my thighs like most men did. But he surprised me.

His dark eyes traveled from my face to my ankles and back again, slower on the way back up. He didn't try to remove my sleep shorts. But it didn't seem to matter. I noticed his breathing change and my gaze dipped to the front of his pants. A telltale bulge, long and thick strained against the fastening. I cleared my throat and took a chance. "If you untie me, I can take care of that for you."

Frowning, he followed my gaze to his swollen cock, like he'd only just noticed it was there. When he met my gaze again, there was a battle in his eyes. Finally, he shook his head. "No."

I arched my eyebrows. "No? I thought you said you liked me."

"Stop, Luna. You don't have to play your sex games with me. They won't get you anywhere."

Shame flooded through me for the first time in years, and once again, hot tears pricked the corners of my eyes. "I'm sorry," I told him. And then I wondered why the hell I was apologizing to this guy who'd broken into Gino's house and restrained me so he could sexually molest me. The next instant, fury flooded through me, my emotions all over the place, and I started to struggle in earnest. "Fucking untie me!"

He ignored me. Sliding his fingertips beneath the waistband of my shorts, he tugged on them.

"No!" I bared my teeth at him. "Stop! Or I swear to god, I'll scream."

"Go ahead," he told me. "I've decided I won't gag you. I like hearing the little noises you make when I touch you. Besides..." He paused what he was doing just long enough to pull a gun from the back of his waistband and check the ammo. Finished, he returned it to its place. "Gino is becoming a problem in the family anyway. His death wouldn't be a great loss, although Luca gets upset with me when I do things outside of his timeline."

Cold air hit my vagina as my shorts were tugged down as far as my wide-spread legs would allow, and I moaned.

I fucking moaned.

CHAPTER 12

Tristan

I waited for her to carry out her threat to scream. Luna was not a woman who went back on her word. I knew this. The fact that she was still here in Gino's house and hadn't tried to escape proved it. Just like I knew she didn't hate my touch as much as she was trying to make me believe she did. It's why I hadn't gagged her yet. I enjoyed the little intakes of breath and other small noises she made as I explored her body.

Not that it mattered. I would touch her even if she didn't like it, just to see what she felt like. But this did make things more...interesting.

Plus, chances were Gino wouldn't come running, even if she did scream. I doubted he'd even hear her. Not over the noise of his CPAP machine and the movie he'd been watching when he'd fallen asleep blaring full blast from his television. And if his guards heard anything, they'd probably assume it was just Gino in here and not dare interrupt.

So, no. I wasn't worried about her screaming. As a matter of fact, I kind of hoped she would.

Luna lay spread out like a buffet for me to eat, and I had to admit, the sight of her made my mouth water. Her dark hair, braided the way she usually wore it at night, lay over her left shoulder, exposing her throat to me. She was beautiful in sleep, but she was even more so with those blue eyes staring up at me in fear. Her lips parted with a gasp as I ran one fingertip over the edge of the triangle of pubic hair that covered the top of her pussy. Even those curls were soft. I wanted to rub my cheek against them.

When I came here tonight, it hadn't been my intention to do this. I'd just wanted to watch her. But when I'd seen her lying there, sleeping so hard, the urge to touch her had grown out of my control. It terrified me, this need I had for her, and yet I couldn't seem to dispel it. I still didn't know why this particular woman had such a hold over me, but at this point, it didn't really matter. It was there, and there was nothing I could do to shake it.

So, I'd given in.

In the top drawer of her dresser with the rest of the silky things she only wore when she dressed for Gino, I'd found two pair of thigh-high silk hose. I used them to restrain her arms and legs. The last thing I wanted to happen would be for her to wake up and strike out in panic, because that could take a nasty turn I'd have little control over. And I really didn't want to hurt her. Accidentally or otherwise.

She started to struggle against the bonds again. She was angry now, and like everything else about her, the range of emotions she'd displayed in the short time I'd been here captivated me. What was it like, to be so controlled by emotions? I watched her for a moment until I was secure in the knowledge she wouldn't escape, then I turned my attention back to the dips and curves of her body.

Her breasts were as fucking close to perfect as any I'd ever seen. I reached toward one, then curled my fingers back. I was almost afraid to touch them. But my curiosity got the best of me, and I squeezed one, manipulating the giving flesh as it overflowed my hand, the hard nipple poking the center of my palm. I did the same to the other breast, comparing them before pinching the hard nipples, rolling them between my fingertips. The entire time, I watched her reaction to my touch, heard the way her breath caught in her chest, and saw the pulse flutter in her throat.

No, she didn't hate my touch.

Luna started to struggle in earnest now, cursing at me, and I placed one hand flat on her lower stomach to hold her still as I took my knife out again. The shorts had to go. They were restricting my explorations. I could wield it with my left hand just as well as my right, and I used this hand to slice through the thin material until there was a good head start. Then I closed it up and put it back in my front pocket, using my hands to finish the job.

When I was done, Luna was completely nude except for the scraps of her tank top laying along either side of her ribcage. Her pale skin shone luminescent through the darkness. Her nipples and dark pubic hair were the only shadows, along with the dip of her stomach just under her naval. She was curvy in clothes, and I saw now that it was her natural figure, not padding or underwires or fancy cuts.

My eyes glued to her naked body, I put one knee up on the bed, quickly becoming obsessed with those curves, and ran my hands, more assertively this time, over the outer sides of her breasts to the dip of her waist and the flare of her hips. My breath came fast and hard as I touched her. My heart pounded, and the blood rushed loudly in my ears. The sensation of so many different curves and textures overwhelming my senses.

Her thighs were on the thicker side, tapering down to her calves and ankles perfectly. I laid my hands over the tops of her legs and spread my fingers. My large hands barely covered the entire width.

Pressing my thumbs into the soft flesh of her inner thighs, I slid them up toward her sex. She stilled as I found the center crease and opened her lips wide. I smelled the earthy musk of her, and I bit my lower lip, wondering what she tasted like.

She'd stopped struggling and now lay waiting to see what I would do. I wanted to see her expression, but I couldn't take my eyes from the delicate pink flesh those dark curls protected. Slowly, savoring the anticipation but too far gone to stop now, I lowered my head and licked her from her ass to her clit.

Luna's hips lurched upward, and she moaned.

My eyes closed so I could savor her taste as my erection grew even more uncomfortable. But I didn't mind the pain. Pain didn't faze me. Most of the time, I barely noticed it. Lowering my body to the bed, I only hesitated for a second before I slid my arms underneath her thighs and reached around her hips, spreading her pussy wide with my fingers. It was a little unnerving with her legs draped over my shoulders, but I was much more interested in having more of this taste. I put my mouth on her again, finding a hard little nub with my tongue.

I sucked her clit into my mouth, then released it, paying close attention to the breathless sounds coming from Luna. Running my tongue lower, I found her entrance and forced my way in before licking my way back to her clit. I took my time, learning every shape, every change in texture, every spot that made her tense until she was writhing on the bed. Well, as much as she could, being tied up with my arms holding her hips to my mouth.

"Tristan...holy fuck..."

Hearing my name said in that way, like she would die if I stopped, even though I could still sense the battle within her and she hadn't given in to me completely yet, did things to me. Strange, wonderful things. A low growl rumbled deep in my chest. I tightened my hold on her, grinding my erection into the mattress. But it wasn't enough. None of this was enough. I wanted to be inside of her.

But first, I wanted to hear her come. Wanted to feel her jerk beneath me. Wanted to taste how much I turned her on. Something I'd never had the privilege of doing before.

A scuff outside the door alerted me two seconds before the door opened. By the time the *stronzo* walked into the room, I was standing inside the closet, hidden by the shadows of Luna's clothes. I took deep, quiet breaths as I forced myself back under control. But the lust turned to red-hot fury as one of Gino's guards, Giulio, found Luna lying on the bed. As I watched, he palmed his cock through his black slacks and smacked his thick lips lewdly.

There'd been no time to cover her up, so she lay on the bed as I'd left her. Naked. Vulnerable. Nipples hard. Her pussy glistening from my mouth. Her breathing fast and harsh and frustrated as she looked around wildly. But as her mind caught up to what was happening and she realized the man standing over her wasn't me, I saw the panic spread across her features as her eyes shot around the room, looking for...

Me.

She was looking for *me* to save her.

I had to forcefully take my eyes from her so I could concentrate on what Giulio was doing. If he tried to touch her, I would kill him. I was tempted to do so anyway, if only for the fact that he'd now seen her naked. And I didn't like that. I didn't like that fucking shit at all.

As a matter of fact, I didn't know how I was going to leave her here now. Whatever had happened up until this point, Luna was mine now. I couldn't leave her here for Gino. Not after I'd felt the soft perfection of her skin and tasted the heat of her pussy.

But now I had another problem, because Giulio had unzipped his pants and had his cock in his hand and was saying shit to Luna that led me to believe he wasn't going to be a gentleman and turn around and leave.

"Gino left you like this?" he asked her. "Wow. I never knew the old man to be such a kinky bastard. Not that I'm complaining." I could hear the lewd grin on his voice, even though his back was to me, and I couldn't see his face. He walked closer to the bed. "I'll tell you what, girl. You keep that pretty mouth of yours shut, and I'll make sure you enjoy what I'm about to do to you."

"Stay the fuck away from me," she hissed at him as she struggled against her bonds.

"Ah, come on, honey. Don't be like that. I know damn well that Gino can probably barely get it up. You'll like this."

Silently, I snuck out of the closet and came up behind him just as he reached out to touch her calf. He started to say something else, but his words were cut off by the belt now wrapped around his throat. My gun would've been more efficient, but it would also leave a mess I didn't have time to clean up.

My eyes met Luna's as Giulio clawed at the belt wrapped around his throat. Her blue eyes were wide and scared, but she didn't utter a sound as I took him down to the floor, wrapped my legs around his, and twisted the belt tighter around my hand. Soundlessly, he struggled against me, spittle running down his chin, fighting for all he was worth until, finally, he stilled. His arm flopped once. His legs twitched. And then he was gone.

Breathing hard, I held him there for a while longer, just to make sure, before I eased myself out from underneath him and pulled the belt free from around his throat. Getting to my feet, I caught my breath while I watched for any signs that he was still breathing. His chest was still and the whites of his partially opened eyes were streaked red with broken blood vessels. I noticed his cock was now soft, like a little worm laying against his thigh.

Dammit. This wasn't what was supposed to happen. But I couldn't very well just stand there and watch while this *stronzo* touched what was mine. And I also couldn't stop him while leaving him alive to rat me out for being here.

Luna was silent and still on the bed behind me. I could barely hear her breathing. When I looked back over my shoulder, she wasn't watching me. Instead, she had her head on the pillow, and she was staring up at the ceiling fan.

I turned my attention back to the body on the floor and sighed heavily. Luca was going to be very angry this time. But he would understand once I explained what happened. He would cover for me, and eventually he would get over it. He always did.

Taking my cell from the outside pants pocket of my right thigh, I tapped the screen and called Milo.

He answered on the second ring. "Hey." We never greeted each other by name.

"Can you meet me?"

"Of course." I heard him moving around. "Do I need to bring anything to get the paint off?"

This is what I liked about Milo. There were never any questions. Not even a surprised tone. His job was to clean up after us, and he did it efficiently and without complaint at any hour. Sometimes, I wondered if the guy ever slept. He never sounded tired when I called. "No," I told him. "But it's the same home."

"Got it. Be there as soon as I can."

"I'll meet you out on the road." I ended the call and put my phone back in my pocket. "I have to go," I told Luna.

She continued to stare up at the ceiling and didn't respond.

As I studied her upturned face, something tugged at my memories, but once again, it wouldn't come to me. Tucking it away to think about at a later time, I stepped over Giulio's leg and approached the side of the bed. "I'm going to untie your hand. Just one. You'll be able to free yourself easily. All I ask is that you wait until I'm out of the room. Can you do that?"

Her jaw clenched.

"Luna? Can you do that?"

Blue eyes met mine but flicked away again before I could read her thoughts. She nodded once.

Pulling out my knife, I sliced through the silk holding her right wrist. She was right-handed. It would be easier for her to untie her other hand this way. Once she was free, I took a step back out of her reach. But I needn't have worried. All she did was lower her arm with a wince, and then waited.

My eyes raked over her naked form one last time before I hoisted the body over my shoulder and opened the window. I threw him outside, then followed, closing the window behind me and replacing the screen.

Next time I had her naked and alone, there would be no interruptions.

CHAPTER 13

Luna

Three days later

I rubbed my wrist as I sat on the bed, waiting for Gino to come tell me he was ready to go. I didn't know why I was doing it. There were no marks from the silk hose. Not anymore. My wrists and ankles had only been slightly red the following morning, and by that night, any discoloration had mostly faded. By the next day, there was no physical evidence at all of what had happened.

But the memories were still there.

Even now, I could feel the wet heat of Tristan's tongue between my legs, just like I was still tied to that bed. I could feel the scruff of his beard and the tickle of his hair on my inner thigh when he tilted his head. The hard, muscular cords of his shoulder and arms holding me in place. I could smell the dark forest scent of him and hear the way he moaned, with surprised pleasure, when he first tasted me.

My pulse picked up, and a delicious throbbing ache began low in my belly that made me want to spread my legs and touch myself. I shifted my weight on the bed, trying to find a position that would give me some relief. I'd been on the precipice of the best orgasm I'd ever had in my life when Gino's guard had walked into my room that night. And my body's reaction to what happened had been unexpected and...

Disturbing.

I tried to tell myself it was just the fear and the fact that there was nothing I could've done to stop him that had my body strung so tight, and it had just naturally transitioned into lust. That's all. Some kind of instinctive animalistic reaction.

You could've screamed. You could've screamed and brought Gino and his guards running.

I pushed the thought away, uncrossing my arms and rising from the bed to pace restlessly around my room. Screaming wouldn't have done me any good. I had no doubt in my mind that had I done that Tristan would've killed them all, instead of just the single guard. He would've started a war when Gino's sons found out. People would've been hurt because of me.

And more importantly, I didn't have access to Gino's money. I would've been left penniless and I'd have to start all over again for me and Logan.

I paused near the window, the near-silent struggles of a man fighting for his life ringing in my ears before I violently shoved the memory away. That sound would haunt me for the remainder of my days, and I was now a witness to a murder for the second time in my life.

What did that mean for me?

There was no way that a man like Tristan would just let me live, knowing I could bring him down at any moment. As had been happening off and on for the last three days, my palms began to sweat, and my chest tightened to the point I felt I could barely breathe. He was going to kill me. That was the only possible outcome of this scenario. I was only surprised that he hadn't done it already.

I forced myself to calm down and think. Maybe there was a way out of this. Tristan was obviously attracted to me. And maybe I was still alive because he'd been interrupted while taking what he wanted from me, and he still wanted to finish what he'd started. Which meant I'd see him again. And *maybe*, if I could prove to him that I'd keep my mouth shut, he'd let me stay alive a while longer. Long enough to convince him not to kill me at all.

I wouldn't let myself feel guilty about how, despite everything, that attraction was reciprocated. Because that meant nothing. It was just a physical reaction between my body and his. Nothing more. And if that attraction would help me make things realistic enough that he didn't kill me, then I would use it, and hope like hell I could keep everything secret long enough to get me out of this mess.

Ignoring my racing pulse, I checked the time. Gino had ordered me to stay here until he came for me. It would be the first time I'd seen him since the day after Tristan had snuck in here. I thought he might ask me about the dead guard, but he hadn't said a word. And now we were going to a dinner party for one of the other family members. A birthday or anniversary or something. I was wearing a simple black dress this time, with my long hair curled into waves, pinned back on one side, and pulled over the opposite shoulder. My shoes were four-inch heels, and the fur wrap he'd gotten me was lying on the bed. I was even wearing the new perfume he'd left in my bathroom at some point. I only wore it when we were going out, so I wasn't sure when he'd made the swap, but I had to admit I liked this new scent a lot more than the other one.

My door opened. But it wasn't Gino who told me to follow him. It was some new guy I hadn't seen before. About my height, with dark hair and eyes and olive-toned skin, he reminded me a bit of a younger Richard Gere. A replacement, I assumed. "Come with me," he ordered, not unkindly, then stepped aside and waited for me to precede him.

Grabbing my fur wrap from the bed and my clutch purse from the top of the dresser, I walked past him into the hall and started toward the front door.

"He's in his office," the new guy informed me.

I stopped at Gino's office door and waited while my escort knocked. At Gino's response to come in, he opened the door for me, stepped aside to let me enter, then closed it behind me, staying out in the hall. Gino was just finishing up a call, so I waited near the door.

As soon as he finished, he stood and buttoned his black jacket. This suit, I noticed, had discreet pinstriping. It reminded me of the old-school mafia guys in the movies. He eyed me with approval as he approached. "I like that dress on you."

"Thank you," I told him, trying to hide my nervousness with a smile.

When he reached me, he leaned in to give me his customary kiss on the cheek, but when he pulled back, he had a strange look on his face. Frowning, he leaned close again and sniffed.

"Do you like it?" I asked him. "I think it suits me a lot better than the other perfume you gave me."

My answer came when he lifted his arm and backhanded me across the face.

I cried out as I felt his ring slice into my cheekbone near the corner of my eye. The force of his blow spun me around, and I wobbled on my heels, dropping my things to catch myself against the wall. I blinked the tears from my eyes, too shocked to move for a few seconds. And when I could, I raised a shaky hand and touched the spot where his ring had cut my cheek, staring in disbelief at the blood on my fingers. Gino had thrown me around once or twice, but he'd never straight-up hit me like this. "What the fuck, Gino?" I yelled. My eye socket throbbed as adrenaline flooded my system. I began to tremble uncontrollably, and the tears I'd tried to blink away rolled down my cheeks, ruining my makeup.

Grabbing me by the hair on the back of my head, he pulled until my back was arched and my toes were barely touching the ground. "No, Luna. I don't FUCKING like it!" Spit sprayed my face, and I closed my eyes.

"Then why did you buy it for me?" I shouted back.

His upper lip curled in a sneer. "I didn't buy you that crap. And I don't know where the hell you got it from, but get rid of it. I don't ever want you to wear it again. You'll wear the perfume I got you and nothing else. Do you understand?"

"But...I..."

"DO YOU FUCKING UNDERSTAND?" He gave my hair another yank.

I winced. "Yes."

He glared at me for another few seconds and then released my hair so fast I would've fallen on my ass if I hadn't grabbed his other arm to steady myself. He shook me off. "Go clean up your face and meet me in the car. You have five minutes. Do NOT make me come after you. Five minutes, Luna. You'll have to shower that shit off later. We're already running late."

I got the hell out of there as fast as I could and rushed past the guard and back down the hall toward my room, releasing a sob of relief when I heard Gino telling the guard to let me go. I needed a moment alone.

It wasn't until I was staring at myself in the bathroom mirror that I allowed the fear that was stuck in my throat to come out on a keening cry that lasted all of three seconds. Gritting my teeth and taking deep breaths, I swallowed down the rest. I didn't have time to process all of this. Not now. Right now, I needed to do as he told me and get my ass out to that car. Later...later, I could fall apart. Not now.

Grabbing my brush, I forced my mind to go blank and fixed my hair. There was a cut near my eye from Gino's ring, and I was pretty sure I'd have a nice bruise tomorrow. Quickly, I pressed a tissue to the cut to stop the bleeding, then, with shaking hands, I covered the redness as best I could with some foundation and cleaned up the mascara smudged beneath my eyes. Taking one last look, I pulled my hair over my face a little more to hide what I could and rushed out of my room and down the hall to the front door, stopping to grab my clutch bag and fur from the floor of Gino's office where I'd dropped them.

Gino didn't say a word to me as I slid into the backseat beside him. He wouldn't even look at me as he pulled out a handkerchief and held it over his face. As soon as my door was closed, the car pulled away from the house. My heart was still pounding from his reaction as I fumbled with the seatbelt, then laid the fur across my lap to give myself something to hang onto as we drove across town.

I didn't let myself think about what had just happened. Wouldn't let him see how shaken I was. Because fuck that. If this was the way Gino was going to treat me, then maybe I didn't need him, or his money, as much as I thought I did. And *nowhere* in our deal did I agree to be his punching bag. As far as I was concerned, his hitting me made our agreement null and void. And as soon as we got to where we were going, I was walking away.

These types of thoughts helped me keep it together until we arrived at the restaurant—a little family-owned place that looked like a cottage straight out of a village in Ireland. The small parking lot was full of cars, so Gino's driver pulled up in front of the entrance to let us out. I pulled my fur around me against the damp chill and climbed out of the car myself as Gino got out the other side and was escorted around by his new guard.

Once he got to where I was, I fell into step behind him and followed him into the restaurant. The inside was exactly what I would have expected. A small foyer filled with knickknacks and photos opened up into three small rooms with tables covered with white lace tablecloths. The wallpaper was old-fashioned white with little green flowers, and the entire place was lit by candles and wall sconces. Very cozy and very charming.

I took all of this in as a lady with a hushed voice and a heavy Irish accent in a flowery dress and pink lipstick greeted us at the entry and took my wrap. We then made our way inside. Gino's attitude swiftly changed from moody to charming as he greeted the other capos and their families.

I followed along behind him, smiling and greeting people on autopilot. The adrenaline rush I'd experienced before was crashing, leaving me feeling shaky and dizzy, all the emotions I'd managed to shove down on the car ride over rising to the surface until it was all I could do not to break down right there in front of everyone.

We made our way around the room until we found the couple celebrating their anniversary—a man and his wife of fifty years whose names I forgot immediately after being introduced. Still, I smiled and made small talk until Gino took over the conversation, then excused myself to go to the restroom while they had him engaged. Weaving my way through the crowd, I found the bathroom down a short hallway and tried to open the door, but I couldn't seem to make my hand work. I started to shake as panic overtook me. "Please. Please," I whispered. I just had to get out of eyesight before I lost it. Why the hell wouldn't my hand work?

A man's hand closed over mine, turned the knob, and opened the door. It was gone as fast as it had appeared, and I was inside the restroom, almost falling over an old-fashioned clawfoot tub in my rush to get away from the curious eyes in the restaurant. I stared at it in surprise until I heard the door close and the click of a lock a second before I heard his voice.

"What the fuck happened to your face?"

Tristan.

My heart sped up for an entirely new reason. Of course, Luca would be here to pay his respects. And where Luca went, so did his guards.

He'd followed me into the ladies' room. I looked up and found my reflection in the mirror. I didn't want him to see me like this. The area around the cut was beginning to swell. Not overly noticeable with all the makeup I had on unless someone looked close enough, but I could see it. And, apparently, so had Tristan. My lower lip began to tremble, and my image blurred behind tears.

"Luna."

With nowhere else to go, I turned toward him. Tristan stood with his back against the door and his dark eyes full of storms.

"What the fuck happened to your face?"

I blinked, willing away the tears that were swiftly building. "Um. Gino. He didn't like my perfume..." I trailed off as my voice caught on a sob. "But he gave it to me," I swore. "He *gave* it to me! Why the hell would he give me perfume to wear that he didn't like?" Where else would it have come from? Was Gino just fucking with me? Why would he do that?

The reality of my situation suddenly hit me full force. It didn't matter either way. I wasn't walking away. I wasn't going anywhere. Gino owned me. I had no control here. He could do whatever the hell he wanted to me. No one would stop him. "It was the perfume," I repeated lamely. I knew I wasn't making any sense.

"Gino hit you?"

His voice was quiet. Controlled. But there was something else there. Something that made me deflate. Something that made me drop the last shreds of the façade I hid behind. Without thinking about what I was doing, I stepped into him, my hands gripping the front of his suit jacket as all the tension and fear and sadness erupted from me all at once. I curled my body against his as I let it all out, staining the front of his expensive suit with my tears.

I didn't notice at first how he stiffened or how his breath caught when I leaned into him, seeking comfort from the only person here who'd shown any concern for me at all. It didn't matter that just a few nights ago, he'd had me tied to my bed while he violated my body. It didn't matter that he'd murdered someone right in front of me. Tonight, he was the one who'd followed me to make sure I was okay.

His hands wrapped around my wrists, and the next thing I knew, he'd spun us around so it was *my* back pressed against the door, and he held both of my wrists in one hand above my head. I felt the rise and fall of his chest against mine as he drew in ragged breaths, his minty breath warm on my cheek. It occurred to me that I'd never smelled alcohol on his breath. But then all of my thoughts fled when he pressed his hips forward, the hard length of him digging into my stomach, and I arched my back without thinking. I knew I shouldn't be encouraging him. But I didn't want to think about what was right and what was wrong. I just wanted to feel.

And Tristan made me feel *good*.

My lips parted and my eyes flew open just in time to see him lower his head until our lips were so close we breathed the same air. His grip on my wrists tightened almost to the point of pain while his other hand slid up the outside of my thigh and over my hip, his fingers digging into my flesh.

Oh, my god. "Please," I whispered.

A low growl rumbled deep within his chest, and then his lips touched mine, salty from my tears. Softly at first, so fucking soft I trembled with the effort to hold still.

No, it wasn't me trembling.

It was him.

Or, maybe it was both of us.

He cursed under his breath, and then his mouth was on mine. He wasn't gentle this time, his sharp teeth nipping at my lips until I gave him full access and his tongue swept into my mouth. Exploring. Tasting. Taking what he wanted.

His kisses weren't made of the practiced maneuvers I was accustomed to from the men who used me. They were raw. Passionate. *Hungry.* Like the only thing driving him was the unhinged need to possess me.

Blood rushed to the surface of my skin until I felt every inch of where his body touched mine, and moisture dampened my silk panties. I moaned, arching into him as much as I could. Madness had overtaken me, but I didn't care. I just wanted to feel his skin against mine. Wanted him to fuck me right here in the bathroom like the whore everyone thought I was.

He shifted, and his thigh pressed between mine. I spread my legs, trying to ease the ache between them, but I needed more. He swallowed the small cry that escaped me, biting my lower lip in warning, and then he was lifting my dress roughly with his free hand.

I almost passed out from pleasure when his fingers found me, sliding beneath the waistband of my panties to find the wet, swollen flesh of my pussy.

He broke off the kiss, his forehead falling to my shoulder and his ragged breathing in my ear as he slid a long, thick finger inside of me.

"Tristan...please." My voice was barely above a whisper as I begged him to finish what he'd started the other night.

His answering groan in my ear was the most erotic thing I'd ever heard. Suddenly, my wrists were free as he dropped to his knees, pulled my panties to the side, and his mouth replaced his fingers. My fingers found his hair for only a second before my hands were grabbed and pressed against the wall on either side of me. I rode his mouth without shame until the tension coiling low in my stomach tightened almost to the point of pain before exploding through me so violently my head smashed into the door behind me, and my legs nearly gave out as wave after wave of pleasure crashed through me.

I pressed my lips together, trying to hold in my cries as Tristan moaned against me, his tongue laving my pussy as I rode out my orgasm. When I could breathe again, I pulled my hands from his and reached for him, wanting to give him the same pleasure he'd just given me.

My fingers had barely grazed his shoulders when he pulled away from me and stumbled to his feet, wiping his mouth with the back of his hand, his dark eyes cold and cautious.

"Don't do that."

It took a moment for the pure terror in his voice to penetrate my own mess of emotions.

Because I don't want you to touch me.

Tristan's words from the other night came back to me. "I'm sorry," I told him. "I'm so sorry. I just wanted to make you feel good, too." Covering my face with my hands, I fought to control myself.

He was quiet for a moment. "Don't cry," he told me. "It's not you."

Turning my back to him, I fixed my panties, pulled down my skirt, and grabbed a handful of toilet paper to wipe my face. I couldn't go back out there looking like this.

"You won't have to worry about Gino hurting you again."

The rage in his voice was surprising. "What does it matter?" I asked him. "Why do you care?"

In the mirror, I saw him tilt his head as though he was seriously considering my question, like it hadn't occurred to him before now to do so. "I don't know," he finally admitted. "But I won't let it happen again."

I laughed. "There's nothing you can do about it. Gino owns me."

"No," he said. "He doesn't. Not anymore."

I didn't have time to stand there and argue with him. Turning to the mirror, I used my fingertips to try to repair the damage to my makeup my emotional breakdown—and his mouth—had caused.

"You look beautiful."

I stilled. He'd said it so quietly I wasn't sure I'd heard him right. "What?"

The door opened and closed, and he was gone.

When I came out a few minutes later, so was Gino.

CHAPTER 14

Tristan

I watched as Luna was escorted out of the restaurant by one of Gino's men. Unfortunately—or rather, fortunately for Gino—he'd been called away by an urgent matter. The matter being that Luca didn't want me to rip out his intestines in front of everyone, so he'd strongly urged him to go home by telling him he'd just gotten word of a threat being made on Gino's life.

Not entirely untrue. The warning had come from Enzo, who'd caught me coming out of the ladies' room and demanded to know what I was up to that was so goddamn important I'd left him alone to watch over Luca. Apparently, "gutting Gino with my bare hands" wasn't the correct answer.

"Come on. We're leaving."

Tearing my eyes from the doorway Luna had just walked through, I nodded to Enzo and went with him as we followed Luca around the restaurant so he could make his excuses for leaving early. I couldn't stand the thought of her going back to that house, and it had taken everything in me not to follow her.

I wet my lips with the tip of my tongue. I could still taste the delicious earthy sweetness of her pussy. When I inhaled, I could smell her perfume on my clothes. A moan caught in my throat. Or maybe not, because Enzo gave me a sideways glance. But I didn't really give a fuck if he heard me. All I knew was I wanted more of that taste, but first I needed to get her away from Gino.

Luca wouldn't look at me when we got into the SUV. When he did, his mouth was drawn into a tight line. "I'm sorry," I told him. "I was off my game tonight, and I left you unprotected." My own frustration with the situation was apparent in my tone, even to me. A get-together like dinner tonight was normally pretty low risk, but Luca was the boss now, and you never knew who might have it out for him. Even within the family.

"You have a job to do," he ground out. "If you can't do that job, let me know, and I'll find someone who fucking can."

He was angry. I could tell by his tone and the tense angles of his posture. "I have no excuse for my behavior," I told him. "But I swear I won't put you in a situation like that again." Seeing Luna's swollen and cut face tonight as she headed to the restroom had caught me by surprise, but that wasn't what made me react without thinking. It was the expression on her face. The panic in her eyes. She'd been on the verge of a complete meltdown. Something that I understood well. And I'd wanted to help her.

"No," Luca said from the backseat. "You won't. Because starting tonight, you're off duty until you figure out whatever the hell is going on with you and that woman."

I twisted around in my seat to look at him. "That's not necessary, Luca."

His blue eyes, as cold and hard as glacial ice, met mine. "Yes, Tristan. It is."

Along with Enzo, I'd been by Luca's side since I was barely a man. But unlike Enzo, I'd been groomed from a young age to protect him with my life without fear. And I would. I fucking *have*. I never thought about any danger to myself. My life wasn't important.

But Luca...he ran this family. He was important, and he needed to stay alive. "I disagree. I can't let you endanger yourself by sending me away. And Enzo can't be there every hour of every day. He has a new wife." A person who might make him think twice before throwing himself in front of a bullet.

"Tristan, you're too distracted, and proved that to me tonight. Even when that woman isn't around, you're thinking about her. Asking questions. She's a mystery you're trying to figure out, and I'm giving you the time to do that. That's all." He sighed, and some of the stiffness left his shoulders. "Look, I get it. I do. When I met Veda... well, you saw how crazy it made me. And I've known you a long time. I know how your mind works. Once you've satisfied your curiosity about her, you can come back to work."

"She's not a curiosity."

"Then what is she?"

"She's..." I paused. I didn't know what she was. But if he was trying to get her out of my head, this wasn't the way to do it. "You do realize that if you take me off duty, I'll have nothing else to do but stalk Luna?" Because I knew that was exactly what I was doing. It wasn't normal. Wasn't an acceptable social behavior. But I'd never given a fuck about that before. I wasn't going to start now.

Enzo broke into our conversation. "He has a point, Luca. You know how Tristan fixates on things that catch his interest. Probably because there's so few things that do." He smirked at me, and I ignored him.

Luca glanced at Enzo, then shifted his attention back to me. "Alright. You're not completely off duty, but you'll stick to the house and doing pickups. If I need to go anywhere, I'll take Enzo and a couple of the other guards. I'm sorry, T, but things aren't very stable within the family right now, and I can't have you in the middle of it while she's around, pulling your attention away. And it looks like she's going to be around for a while."

"*Capisco*," I told him. I did understand. I didn't like it, but he was right. Like he'd said, I'd proven tonight that my "curiosity" with Luna would only put him in unnecessary danger. And that couldn't happen.

"All I'm asking," Luca continued, "is that you're careful. And that you stay away from Gino."

"That will be hard," I told him honestly. "Considering the circumstances."

"It will be. But I'm telling you, as your boss, to leave him alone. And do not allow him to find out about this...thing you have with his property. Don't look at me like that. You know damn well that's what she is."

He was right. But it still rubbed me wrong to hear it said out loud.

"Promise me, Tristan."

I shifted my gaze to the window and watched the city go by as I struggled with my response. I wanted to tell him what he wanted to hear, but it would be a lie. I've told him untruths before, but never about something that could come back to bite him in the ass. "I can't do that," I finally said. "But I swear, I will only harm Gino as a last resort and not without telling you first." It was the only promise I was willing to make.

I looked back to find him staring at me. A muscle twitched in his jaw at my direct disobedience. But I couldn't lie to him. Not about this. Finally, he gave me a nod. "I guess that's all I can ask," he conceded.

The rest of the ride home was thankfully silent, which gave me plenty of time to be in my head. And the only thing in there with me was Luna. I couldn't stop thinking about her. Why, out of all the people in the world, was this woman the one who'd dug into my brain like a maggot? Why did my body ache for her like she was the oxygen I needed in my blood?

I had no answer for any of this, but I was hoping that whatever the fuck this was would play itself out eventually, and things would go back to normal. *I* would go back to normal.

However, at this moment, all I could do was wonder what she was doing right now. Had she made it back to Gino's? Was she safe? Was she alone in her room, or was Gino in there with her? My skin grew hot, and my stomach twisted at the thought. Restlessly, I shifted in my seat, my fists clenched in my lap, and focused on our conversation in the bathroom to distract myself.

She'd told me Gino had struck her because he was upset about the perfume I'd brought her. Personally, I thought it was perfect for her. Although I *had* questioned my decision after getting her alone in the restroom and discovering how delicious that particular scent was once it warmed on her skin. But the bigger question was, why had Gino gotten so upset over something as simple as what perfume she wore?

I had to wonder if he suspected something. It wouldn't be entirely out of the question. Perhaps it had been stupid of me to replace the perfume when there was no way Luna could've gotten it herself. In my desire to get rid of that other horrid flowery shit she had, I'd acted impulsively. I mulled over that possibility as I checked the mirrors to confirm no one had followed us, but then I quickly dismissed it. Gino was short-tempered and had an over-inflated ego. If he knew I was sneaking into his home to take something—or someone—he considered his property, there's no way in hell Luca wouldn't have heard about it by now. Hell, I'd shown an interest in Luna right in front of him, and I'd killed two of his guards. If he'd connected the two, there's no way in hell he would be able to stay quiet about it.

So, no. I didn't think he suspected me. However, I was morbidly curious to know where he thought his two missing guards had suddenly gone.

Once we got Luca home safe to Veda, who had skipped tonight's celebration because she wasn't feeling well, he dismissed me for the night with a look of warning. One that I didn't heed. I needed to check on Luna and make sure she was okay before I'd be able to get any sleep tonight.

And perhaps make her come again so I could dream of her breathless cries and the way she said my name.

My mouth suddenly went dry. What would it feel like to come inside of her? Her mouth. Her pussy. Her ass. Everywhere. I wanted to tie her up again and finish what I'd started the other night. I wanted to fight the terrors of my past, crawl inside of her, and wear her skin as my own. Feel her blood flow through my veins, and our hearts beat in sync until it was just the two of us and her sweet heat thawed the ice inside of me. And maybe then, when I'd experienced her inside and out, I'd get her out of my system.

Her bedside lamp was still on when I arrived outside her window. Luna was there in her room, sitting on the edge of her bed with her head bowed. She'd changed out of the dress and was wearing a white T-shirt, but her back was to me, so I couldn't see what she was doing. I should've brought her something to eat. She was rushed out of the restaurant so fast I knew she didn't have a chance to get anything. And I would bet my life that Gino hadn't given her a second thought.

I listened for any sign of movement around me, but there was nothing more than the rustling of leaves and the drip of moisture from the roof. Turning back to the window, I pulled the screen off, hiding it behind the bushes so it wouldn't be noticed, eased the glass pane open, and climbed in.

When I straightened to my full height, Luna stood near the end of her bed, watching me with her large blue eyes. Her cell phone was in her hand, but it was hanging at her side and the screen was black. "Turn off the lamp," I ordered quietly.

Her eyes flicked to the open window before coming back to me, and her thoughts were written all over her face. She was wondering how many times I'd gotten into her room in precisely this manner without her knowing about it. I waited, allowing her to sort through it all. After a long moment, she walked over and switched off the light.

Once the room was dark enough that I wouldn't be illuminated to anyone who might wander by outside, I closed the window and approached her. When I was close enough to touch her, I stopped, my eyes sweeping over her lush body. Luna was soft and curvy and made for fucking. Closing my hands into fists, I breathed in her sweet, womanly scent. I loved the way she smelled. Along with the white shirt, she'd put on a pair of soft-looking black leggings. She still had her makeup on, and I had the sudden urge to smear the lipstick across her face with my cock. Her feet were bare, toes painted red, and her luscious hair was pulled back in a ponytail.

She was beautiful. There was no denying it. But that wasn't all that attracted me to her. I sensed a strength inside of her, something older than her years that haunted her blue eyes even when she smiled and called to my own broken spirit. I swayed toward her, longing to feel her against me so much I could barely breathe, to hold her so close that our two broken souls would meld and become whole.

Yet, the thought of her hands on me made my blood run cold. When she'd fallen into me at the restaurant, the instinct to strike out at her had been just as strong as my need to run, and for a few seconds, I couldn't move. It was only when I'd had her under my control that the feeling of her soft curves against me had sent me spiraling into a lustful need so powerful I'd nearly come right then and there. I'd managed to hold myself in check. Barely. But I didn't want to do that now. I wanted to taste her again. "Take your hair down."

She shook her head. "No. You can't keep coming here like this, Tristan. You need to leave."

Why was she arguing with me? She'd enjoyed what I'd done to her at the restaurant. She'd pleaded with me to make her come, and I had. I wanted to make her come again. "I came to make sure you were okay."

"Then why do I need to take down my hair?"

"Because I want to touch it. And I want to taste you again."

She stilled and sucked in a breath. "I don't want you to do that."

"Yes," I countered. "You do." She shook her head again, but she was lying. If she didn't want me here, she wouldn't be standing in front of me with her lips parted and her gorgeous breasts rising and falling with every quick, nervous breath. That phone in her hand would be calling Gino, and she would've screamed for help the moment she saw me coming in the window.

"Look," she started. "What happened at the restaurant... I'm sorry. It should never have gone that far. I was just... really upset. And you were there. And I just needed to feel like someone cared—"

I cut her off. "Don't lie to me."

Her mouth snapped shut. She didn't bother to defend herself. "Tristan, if Gino finds you here—"

I nodded toward her phone. "Call him if you don't want me here."

Looking down at the phone in her hand, she frowned, like she'd forgotten it was there.

I took half a step closer, reached behind her, and pulled the band from her hair. Long, soft tendrils of dark hair spread across her back and tickled the back of my hand. Gathering a handful in my fist, I closed my eyes and buried my nose in the soft, fragrant strands. "Never cut your hair," I ordered.

When I opened my eyes, I saw her reaching toward my chest. Dropping her hair, I took a hurried step back. "Don't do that."

She blinked at me, then little creases appeared between her eyebrows. "Why not?"

"I don't like to be touched."

"But you touch me."

"Because I need to. I don't like it when *you* touch *me*." I didn't mind sharing this with her. It was better for her to know the rules.

"Oh," was all she said. Then, "Why not?"

"That's a story I'd rather not tell tonight."

She tilted her head slightly with curiosity, but she didn't push it.

I stepped toward her again. "I need to taste you again, Luna. Please." My voice had gone low and husky, but I couldn't help it. I craved her like I craved air.

She didn't give me permission, but she didn't move away as I closed the rest of the distance between us. Her blue eyes held me mesmerized as I shrugged off my jacket and laid it on the bed, then removed my pistol and shoulder harness, leaving it within easy reach. I'd already left my tie in the SUV.

I unbuttoned the top buttons of my shirt, then froze, remembering what was hidden beneath the material, and dropped my hands. I didn't know how she would react to my scars, and I didn't want anything to distract her right now.

Her eyes dropped to the skin I'd revealed, but before she could see anything, I took her face in my hands. "Don't touch me," I ordered right before I took her lips with mine.

She tasted like sweet red wine, and I drank her in, even as I realized this was why she'd been so calm when I'd broken into her room. I kissed her lips, her jaw, the pulse in her throat... I kissed her until our hearts were racing and Luna trembled beneath my hands. "I want to fuck you," I confessed. "God, I want to fuck you. But not here," I told her when she whimpered. "Not now." Then I stepped away. I had to. My self-control was rapidly slipping.

Luna swayed before me, her lips swollen from my kisses, and her hands fisted at her sides. She didn't protest when I stopped, but I could see the internal battle she fought in her eyes. I'd grown to know the way her mind worked and the kind of woman she was. And right now, she felt guilty for wanting me when she'd sworn to Gino that she would be loyal to him.

To distract myself from my raging hard-on, I checked out the swelling around her eye. "How is your face?" It was hard to see in the dim light from the bathroom if the swelling had gotten any worse.

"It's fine," she told me a bit breathlessly.

"Why did he hit you?"

"I told you why."

I stared at her until she started talking again. "He apologized to me when I got home."

This is not your fucking home. The thought surprised me, but I had no time to ponder it as she continued talking.

"He apologized," she repeated. "And explained to me that he'd only gotten so angry because the perfume he'd bought for me was the same kind his dead wife had worn. And he...he missed her so much and how he'd been so lonely. He said I remind him of her. And that was why he wanted me to wear it. He's buying me more since I can't find the other bottle."

Wait.

Something tugged at the edge of my mind again. A memory that scattered as soon as it started to become cohesive. I watched Luna as she continued talking, telling me how Gino had teared up and groveled, begging her for her forgiveness. I studied the curve of her cheek. The line of her jaw. The slight slant of her eyes. Her pale skin and the way she gestured when she talked.

God fucking dammit.

The memory that had been evading me suddenly exploded in my head, clear as day. I knew why she seemed so familiar to me.

My blood chilled as events that happened seventeen years ago slammed through me. Things I wanted to forget, but never could. The dots were all connecting. And if I was right...Jesus, if I was right...

Fear for her twisted my bowels, another long-forgotten emotion. One I hadn't felt since I was a child. My mind raced as I shoved that fear down deep into the emotional lockbox I'd created out of necessity for my own survival. And now it would come in handy for Luna's. I needed to be sure that what I suspected was true, though, before I acted on it. "I'm sorry, I need to go." Quickly, I strapped on my holster and grabbed my jacket from her bed.

"What? Wait! Where are you going?" She followed me to the window.

"Stay here. Lock your door," I told her. I allowed myself the luxury of looking back at her and memorizing her features one more time before I turned and opened the window. "Take this. Use it if you have to." Reaching into my front pants pocket, I pulled out the small knife I carried on me at all times. I would've left her my gun, but I would need that if I was caught sneaking back off the property. "I'll be back," I promised.

With one last brush of my lips to hers, I slipped outside.

CHAPTER 15

Luna

I laid in bed for hours waiting for Tristan to come back, my mind spinning and my fingertips lightly touching my bruised lips, the knife he'd left with me tucked under my pillow.

What the hell was I doing? What was I thinking?

I needed to get my shit together and stop swooning over a mafia guy I knew absolutely nothing about except that he could make me come like nobody's business.

He also killed for you.

My fingers stilled, and I dropped my hand back to the bed near my hip. That knowledge was more seductive than his kisses, I had to admit. Was that why I didn't tell Gino about him? Why I reacted to him the way I did? Why my body was on fire for him even now? Other than my brother, I'd never known anyone who cared enough about me to protect me from anything.

Hell, I'd half expected to come home to an empty house tonight after Tristan's parting words at the restaurant. The guard who was waiting for me when I left the bathroom had put me in an empty car for the ride home, and it wasn't until I got to the house and found Gino drinking in his office that I knew he was still alive. I'd smiled through my disappointment and accepted the glass of wine he'd handed me, along with his apology. Then I'd taken a second glass of wine. And a third.

He didn't scold me for hiding in the bathroom at the party. Instead, he drank along with me and started telling me about his dead wife. When his stories became stilted and his sentences trailed off, I'd fully expected him to fuck me. He always did when he drank like that. And when he didn't, I started to worry that he would follow me to my room to do it. For the first time in a long time, shame and disgust had rolled through me, hoping that Tristan would show up, but not wanting him to see Gino using my body.

What would he do if he saw Gino fucking me through the window again? Would he watch like he had before? Or would he sneak into my room and kill him while he was still inside of me?

But to my surprise, Gino had smiled at me, smoothed my hair with his hand like I was a child, and sent me off to bed after telling me he'd see me in the morning. Glad to escape, I'd stumbled down the hall to my room and gotten changed. Then I'd sat on my bed and waited, much like I did now, for the man I knew would come.

My plan was to tell him this...*thing* between us had to stop. That I belonged to Gino. I'd made an agreement with him, and I was going to live up to my end. My brother's future depended on it. *My* future depended on it. I had to stop messing around like this.

And what about the guard he'd killed? Tristan had given no indication that he was even the slightest bit concerned about my being a witness to the murder he'd committed right here in my room, and I was beginning to believe that he genuinely wasn't. As a matter of fact, he didn't seem like a man who was concerned about much of anything except getting what he wanted when he wanted it, especially when it came to me.

However, when he'd shown up, his jaw tense and his dark eyes burning with lust, the words had dried up in the back of my throat, and I couldn't recall the speech I'd prepared so carefully in my head.

I sighed and rolled over, putting my back to the door and facing the window. Then I threw off the blankets. A minute later, I was too cold and pulled them back over my legs again. My braid felt too tight, so I tugged on the strands until it wasn't pulling my scalp, remembering how Tristan had gathered the mass of it in his hands and pulled it up to his nose. Then I had an itch in the middle of my back that I couldn't reach, and it wouldn't go away, so I got up and went into the bathroom. Grabbing my comb off the sink, I tried to reach it that way for a few seconds before I gave up and used the corner of the wall. Then I got back into bed and went back to watching the window.

My stomach growled, and I sighed. I hadn't eaten much of anything today, and I'd been too upset to think about it when I'd gotten back here tonight. Rolling over, I stared at the door. It wasn't locked. At least, not that I knew of. And Gino had drunk enough wine that I was pretty positive he'd be passed out by now. I could probably sneak down to the kitchen and find something to eat.

Then I rolled back over and faced the window again, worried that if Tristan returned and I wasn't in here, he'd start searching the house for me. And what if he ran into Gino or one of the guards? What if they hurt him? Or worse? If I was being real, it was hard to imagine anyone who would be able to get close enough to that man to harm him without him knowing about it. But they had guns. You didn't need to be close to someone to shoot them.

Closing my eyes, I tried to settle down enough to go to sleep, but all I could see was Tristan standing in my room, his jacket off and his shirt unbuttoned, showing off a strong chest with naturally tan skin and a light dusting of dark hair. I'd also seen what he'd obviously been trying to hide—the pink and white, puckered scars that peeked out from beneath the edges of his shirt. I wondered how many of those scars he had.

I don't like to be touched.

I heard the creak of a floorboard out in the hall, interrupting my thoughts. My door opened, and I rolled over to find Gino standing half in and half out of my room.

"I thought you'd be asleep," he told me.

For a moment, I couldn't speak over the pounding of my heart. In the weeks that I'd been here, Gino had always been pretty predictable in his actions. And he'd never shown up in my room after sending me to bed. He either came with me immediately, or he didn't show up at all. At least, that I knew of. Had he been coming to my room when I was asleep? Exactly how many men had been creeping around my room at night? "Um, no. Not yet."

"May I come in?"

I didn't answer him because I didn't really think my answer would've mattered, and he didn't seem to expect one as he stepped the rest of the way in and shut the door behind him. He turned back toward me, and I caught a flash of metal caught in the dim glow from the bathroom nightlight. Slowly, I pushed myself up to a sitting position. Despite my racing heart, I managed to keep my voice calm. "Gino? What's going on?"

Using the barrel of the gun in his hand, he scratched his head, then let it drop back down to his side. "I've loved you for a long time, Luna. A long, long time." His words were slightly slurred.

I laughed nervously, trying to lighten the situation and tease him into a better mood. "We haven't known each other that long, Gino."

He scrubbed his face with his free hand. "You don't understand."

"Then why don't you explain it to me?" I just needed to keep him talking long enough to give me time to think. He was obviously very drunk. He must've kept drinking after I'd left him in his office.

He shook his head. "I can't."

"Why not?"

"Because you'll hate me. You'll think I'm a monster after what I've done."

I already thought he was a monster. Sometimes. But I wouldn't say I hated him. "Indifferent" was a better term. Pulling the blankets back, I slid my legs over the side of the bed. I'd changed into my usual sleeping clothes after Tristan left, a tank and sleep shorts, and I planned to use my skimpy attire to my full advantage. If I could distract Gino with my body, maybe he'd put that damn gun down and sober up enough to come back to his senses. "I'd never hate you, Gino. Why would you think that? You've done nothing but take care of me and my family."

His eyes fell to my breasts hanging free beneath my shirt. I'd never been so glad that I'd chosen my thinnest shirt to wear tonight. It was also such a light pink it was practically see-through. Of course, it wasn't Gino I'd had in mind when I'd chosen it.

My feet touched the floor, and I spread my legs slightly and thrust my chest out. Nothing too obvious. Just enough to keep his attention. "Why would you think that, Gino?"

His eyes dropped to my crotch, then quickly rose to my face. "Because I shouldn't be looking at you like this."

"Why not? I like the way you look at me."

He frowned. "No, you don't. You fight me."

I didn't bother to deny it. "I thought you liked it when I fight you."

His forehead creased in confusion. "I do."

"There's nothing wrong with that. It's exciting."

The barrel of the gun was now rubbing the bulge in his pants. I didn't think he was even aware of it. I got to my feet slowly, careful not to make any sudden moves as I closed the distance between us. "Why don't you let me help you with that?" Pushing the gun out of the way with a shaking hand, I started to undo the fastening of his slacks.

He let me do it, his lips parting on a loud inhale as I dropped to my knees in front of him and pulled out his semi-hard cock. Keeping my eyes wide and innocent, I looked up at him as I sucked the head into my mouth.

"I've loved you for so long," he repeated, watching me.

He still held the gun in his hand, and I watched it out of the corner of my eye, wishing I'd remembered to grab the knife. I had no idea if he'd come in here planning to kill me or himself or both of us, but I couldn't panic. If I did, this wasn't going to end well. But maybe, just maybe, if I could get him out of this mood he was in, he'd change his mind.

With one hand, I held the base of his shaft, and with the other, I cupped my breast, lifting it and playing with my nipple through the material of my shirt. I moaned as I sucked him in deep. His dick wasn't tiny, but it wasn't overly large either, and I could easily take all of him in. I scraped my teeth along the sensitive skin as I released him, feeling him swell and harden.

I gave the best damn blowjob of my life, and soon I felt his hand on the back of my head, guiding me as he started slamming his cock into my mouth, his breathing harsh and uneven. Closing my eyes, I concentrated on not gagging and silently hoped he'd pass out when he finished so I could get the gun away from him.

"Yes, baby. I'm gonna fucking come...I'm gonna co..." I opened my eyes, and his words broke off as they met his stare. His face crumpled, and cold, hard metal dug into my temple. "Jesus, help me," he whispered.

I broke out into a cold sweat, fear twisting my gut, and froze with his dick still in my mouth.

"Give me strength," he continued. "Please, give me strength." He rocked his hips slightly, and I watched as tears filled his eyes and rolled down his cheeks.

My mind spun. I was going to die. I could see it in his eyes. I was going to die because of Gino's sudden Catholic guilt. Why? Because we weren't married? Or because he'd bought me like a whore?

A frightened sob slipped out of me as he continued to fuck my mouth, harder again now, his fingers tightening in my hair as the barrel of the gun dug into my temple. I felt him swell in my mouth as his orgasm neared.

Suddenly, his eyes hardened with determination. "I'm sorry, sweet girl," he panted. "I'm so sorry. I'm a sick, sick man. It isn't your fault. But this is for the best."

No. No, it fucking wasn't.

I bit down as hard as I could. At the same time, I knocked the gun away from my head. A shot rang out, emphasizing Gino's scream of pain as he fell back against the door and tried to rip my mouth off his dick by my hair. Blood covered my tongue, and I opened my mouth, falling on my ass as I frantically tried to spit it out.

Gino writhed in pain in front of me, both hands covering his crotch and the gun still in his hand. I had to get the fuck out of there. If he didn't shoot me, one of the guards who were surely heading this way would. As if on cue, someone slammed into my bedroom door, trying to open it, but Gino's heavy girth was blocking it.

"Gino? Gino!"

I scurried to my feet and ran to the window. Tears ran down my cheeks, and I was shaking so hard it took me three tries to get the window open. The screen practically fell out when I pushed on it, and I dove after it, falling to my knees in the rocky dirt. A shot rang out, hitting the tree in front of me about two feet above my head, and I screamed. Rising to my feet, I ran blindly. Rocks and burs stuck into my bare feet, and I didn't know where I was going, but I ran like the hounds from hell were after me, Gino's angry shouts echoing in my ears.

Giving the house a wide berth, I circled around to the front. There was a road here. There had to be. I didn't feel the cold air on my bare skin or the pain in my feet. I didn't feel anything except the pounding of my heart and the rush of blood in my ears. I didn't know if anyone was following me. Looking back would only slow me down.

My breath sawed in and out of my chest. Almost there. I was almost there. I just had to get to the road and find a neighbor's house or flag down a passing car or something.

My forward flight was suddenly halted when a steel band wrapped around my waist, and I was hauled back against a hard chest. "No!" I cried out. Kicking and punching, I fought them. I'd been so fucking close! "Let me go!"

There was a sharp pain in my neck, and I felt something cold flood my veins. The world went fuzzy around me, and my arms and legs suddenly weighed a thousand pounds. "Let me go," I whispered. I caught the scent of the forest at night right before my vision went black and the world faded away.

CHAPTER 16

Tristan

Earlier that night...

I hated leaving Luna there, but if I'd taken her...no, *when* I took her...that boat with Gino in it that Luca was so fucking concerned about was going to capsize and burst into flames before it sank so deep it would never be found again. And there'd be no saving it. Especially if what I suspected was true.

The burn of chains flogging the skin of my back and ass, even my thighs. The taste of my own blood filling my mouth as men I was taught to respect threw out degrading taunts with each hit, trying to get me to react...

Giving my head a shake, I tried to throw off the memories. But still, they came. One after another, as I struggled to stay in my lane on the highway and get myself home. Memories that led up to something I'd done seventeen years ago. Something that had to do with Luna.

"Are you a boy? Or are you a man?"

"Neither. You're nothing. Do you hear me? Nothing. You don't matter..."

I wiped the sweat out of my eyes with the back of my hand. I didn't want to think about the trials I was put through as a child, but sometimes they were just...there. Reminders of how I became the man I am today. A man who doesn't think twice about putting himself in harm's way if it will protect the ones who are truly important. A man who knows his place in this world.

Cramps twisting my stomach until I bend over in pain. My heart racing, and yet I'm so weak I can barely crawl across the room...

Swerving at the last minute, I barely missed the cement divider in the middle of the road.

Hands reaching for me. Cutting me. Burning me. Hitting me.

Touching me in places a man should never touch a boy.

No one touched me now. Not anymore. The last man who had, laughing like it was a joke when I told him not to do it, only had one hand now.

And he wasn't laughing anymore.

My teeth began to hurt, but I couldn't unclench my jaw. The pain gave me something to focus on, something besides the glimmers of my past that darted through my head. I wished I had my knife. I kept the blade dull so it would hurt more when I dug the tip into my skin, but it was sharp enough to pierce a man's ribs if needed. I didn't use it on myself much anymore, preferring instead to try to ride out these episodes until they passed. But I didn't have time for that shit tonight.

I slammed both palms down on the steering wheel so hard it jarred my bones and chased away the memory that had been trying to form. Another tried to take its place, but I concentrated on Luna's face. Her voice. The feel of her skin and her hair. Memories of her chased away the ghosts of my past, and she kept me grounded enough that I didn't run off the road.

A few minutes later, I pulled up to my house and parked the SUV. I could still see lights on in the main house. Pulling out my cell, I called Luca as I walked through my front door. "I'm sorry to bother you this late, but this is important. Can you walk over here? And come alone, please." He would be safe outside the walls of his house. Unlike Gino, Luca's property was very well guarded.

"I'm on my way."

"Thank you. The door is open. I'll be in my office."

The house I occupied on Luca's compound was tiny compared to the main house, but it was plenty big for me.

It consisted of a kitchen, a living room with a couch, a padded rocking chair, a large television I never watched, an office, a bedroom, and the guest room—which contained the cell I used when I needed to escape from the world. The room I kept locked whenever I wasn't in there.

I knew it wouldn't take Luca long to get here, so I didn't waste any time pulling up the file on Luna and her brother he'd sent me. I stared at the pictures of the two of them, not wanting to believe my suspicions. Scrolling through the report, I searched for any other photos, perhaps from when they were children.

Checking the camera feed where I monitored the grounds, I saw Luca approach my front door and let himself in. He was still in his business suit, which meant he'd still been working when I called. "What's going on?" he asked when he reached my office.

I didn't respond at first. I couldn't. I was looking at the photos of Luna and her brother I'd just pulled up from seventeen years ago when they were put into the foster system.

Goddamn it. I was right. A sick feeling soured my stomach and bile rose in my throat.

"Tris? What is it?"

Without looking at him, I asked, "Do you remember the woman your father had me kill seventeen years ago? Right before I was officially placed in your service?" I remembered her. How could I not? She was the first life I'd ever taken. And she'd put up one hell of a fight. Added some interesting scars to my collection.

He thought about it for a second. "She was Gino's wife. And a rat. My father found out she was working with the feds. What about her?"

"She and Gino had two children together. A boy and a girl. Did you never wonder what happened to those children?"

I saw the pieces clicking together in his mind. He knew. He fucking knew.

"What happened to those children, Luca?"

"They were given up for adoption," he responded. His voice sounded far away, caught in the past with me. "Gino gave them up, I assumed, in a gesture of loyalty to my father when he told him to get rid of them because they had their mother's dishonest blood. I remember him bragging about it at dinner that night, how his capos would do anything for him, even give up their own flesh and blood."

"I saw those children when I killed their mother."

That had his attention. "What? You never told me that."

"I never told anyone. They were witnesses. If I had, Luigi would've had them killed." Going back to my computer, I found what I was looking for. Two photos. One of Luna and the other of her brother, Logan. The caption told me she was nine at the time, her brother five. Slowly, I stood, my eyes never leaving the large blue eyes of the girl.

Luca came around my desk and pointed at the screen. "It's not the same children. Their surname is Wilde, not Ricci."

No. It was them. I knew it was the same children all the way down to my bones. Walking over to the generic painting hanging on the wall to my left, I moved it out of the way and opened the safe hidden behind it. This was my decoy safe. I didn't keep anything of much importance in there. At least, nothing that couldn't be replaced. The real safe was in my bedroom, hidden underneath the floorboards in my closet.

Inside, there was nothing but a stack of photos and a few other odds and ends. I removed the photos, pulling out the one on the very bottom and returning the rest to the safe. I took it to Luca and handed it to him.

"What is this?" he asked.

He knew what it was, but I answered him anyway. "It's a photo of my first kill. Your father gave me this to make sure there would be no mistakes, and I kept it. I kept all of them." I pointed at the woman in the photo. She was outside, standing beside a black car, wearing a nice pair of jeans and a blouse. Her long, dark hair—so dark it was nearly black—was pulled back from her face, and her blue eyes squinted against the sun. And she was smiling. "That's Gino's wife. And that,"—I moved my finger to the young girl standing beside her—"is Luna. The same girl in that report who was put into foster care with her brother. This one." I pointed to a five-year-old Logan. "Their last name was changed and they were lost in the system, like so many other kids."

"What you're implying is impossible," he told me as he stared between the two photos. "If Gino is her father, how does she not remember him? She was old enough to know him."

With an impatient shrug, I said, "She saw her dead mother lying on the ground and then her father gave her away. Maybe she blocked it out." When he continued to keep looking back and forth between the photos, I walked away. I was done waiting.

"Tristan, where are you going?"

"To get more guns. I'm taking her out of there."

"Tristan. Stop."

My body reacted to the command despite the panic in my blood. Spinning on my heel, I turned to face him. "What?" I bit out.

He narrowed his eyes at my tone, but didn't call me out on it. Sliding his hands into his front pockets, he began to pace the length of my office. "We can't remove her right now, T. Not now."

"Why the fuck not?"

"Because he's her father. And she's not a child. Whatever their relationship, it's none of our business."

I'd like to say I was surprised by the words coming out of Luca's mouth, but honestly, I wasn't. He'd always been able to push aside his emotions and do what had to be done to advance himself in the organization and to protect those he cared about. Except when it came to Veda. He lost his shit when it came to her. "This isn't just my suspicion here, Luca. I saw him *fucking* her with my own eyes. His own fucking daughter!"

At my outburst, his eyes flew to mine. "Perhaps he doesn't realize she's his daughter. Just like you didn't remember who she was until tonight."

But I shook my head. "He knows." It all made sense now. The way he'd been treating her. How he'd locked her in her room. Starved her. It was his own guilt eating him alive.

Luca looked away, and his eyes narrowed on some point in the distance. "Why would he bring her out to family functions? Parading her around on his arm that way. Surely, he had to know that someone would recognize her, eventually."

"Because everyone who knew her mother is now dead. Who is left to accuse him of incest? Your *padre* and your *fratello* were perhaps the last ones, as they were both there when Luigi gave me the order to kill her. The younger ones in the family were kept out of it. Once

Mario was dead and Enzo took out your *padre*, there was no one to stop Gino from doing what he wanted."

"What about us? We were there. We knew her. Why isn't he concerned about us?"

"I don't know. Maybe because he doesn't plan on us being around long enough to out him. Or he thinks we weren't around her enough to remember. I'd only ever seen her once before I was ordered to kill her. Probably the same with you and Enzo."

Luca stared at me. "Perhaps you're right."

"I know I'm right. What I don't understand is why we're still standing here discussing this."

He held up a hand, palm out. "Before you go running off, tell me, has he hurt her in any way?"

"He *fucked* her. More than once. And he hit her."

"But did he seriously hurt her? Luna is a grown woman who has been a sex worker for a long time. She knew what she was getting herself into when she made this deal."

"SHE DIDN'T KNOW SHE'D BE FUCKING HER OWN FATHER!" Pain shot through my head, and I squeezed my eyes shut and slammed my hands to my temples. Jesus fucking Christ. Why was he arguing with me?

Luca didn't say anything for a long moment, and I knew he was as shocked as I was at what I'd just done. Although he and Enzo often got into heated arguments when they disagreed, I always did what I was told and never gave him any shit about it. However, that was because I never cared one way or the other about what he was asking me to do. This time, though...this time, I cared. I didn't know why. Didn't know what it was about her that brought this out in me or how she managed to burrow so deep under my skin. And I didn't fucking like it. Or know how to handle all the emotions spinning around inside of me. But it was what it was. And I couldn't leave her there so Gino could do to her what he'd done to...

I cut off the thought.

When Luca did finally speak, he kept his tone calm and even. "Even if that were true, it's not our concern. What Gino does or doesn't do with his long-lost daughter is his business. Not ours." As I stared at him in disbelief, he began to pace again. "But perhaps we can use this to draw him out. You know as well as I that he's just biding his time. He's up to something. And I believe he's planning to come after me. After us, Tristan. We have to be prepared. And going after Luna all half-cocked will only give him the upper hand." He stopped pacing directly in front of me and looked me in the eye. "Do you agree?"

Logically, yes. He was right. Gino was playing the long game. "Yes. Gino wants to remove you, but he needs to do it the right way so the family won't dispute his claim to be boss."

"Are you willing to let that happen?"

"No. Of course not."

"Good. Then Luna stays with Gino. For now," he added. Decision made, he walked around me and headed to the door.

"I could kill him." It was an easy solution.

He stopped and turned back toward me. "You could. But I don't think Gino is acting alone in this. I need him alive, for now, to draw out whoever the hell has the balls or the stupidity to team up with him. She'll be okay, Tristan. She's a smart girl. A survivor." With those parting words, he was gone, feeling confident that, as always, his order would be followed.

I waited until I heard the front door open and close, and then I put the picture of Luna's mother back in the safe. I didn't want her to find it. Not just yet. Although I would show it to her, eventually. I didn't want there to be any secrets between us.

Walking over to the camera feed, I watched Luca walk back to his house. When I was sure he was inside, I took out my cell phone and called a contact of mine. "I need something that will knock someone out for at least a few hours. Yes. Yes. A woman. And I need it tonight." I gave him her approximate weight.

Once we had a meeting place, I ended the call and left my office. I needed to change and prepare the spare bedroom.

I would deal with the consequences when they came, but Luna was not spending one more night in that place.

CHAPTER 17

Luna

I rose from the depths of a sticky black bog in gradual waves, like I was swimming through molasses, but I couldn't seem to open my eyes. They were so heavy, like they had weights on them or were taped shut or something.

My heart sped up, and I touched one eyelid with my fingertips just to make sure I could still move. I could, and there was nothing over my eyes.

Giving in to the blackness, I drifted back to sleep.

The next time I woke, a bright light burned through my eyelids, hurting my eyes. I rolled over onto my back with a groan, my right hip and shoulder aching. When the hell did this bed get so hard?

"Don't panic. You're alright."

The voice came from my right, startling me. My eyes flew open, and I blinked rapidly, trying to focus as my pupils adjusted to the light coming from a lamp in the corner. I struggled to sit up, but the muscles in my arms and legs didn't seem to want to work. I rolled back over to my side.

"You're groggy because you were drugged. The effects will wear off completely in another hour or so. I had to do it in order to get you here safely. I couldn't take the chance of you alerting Gino or his guards, even accidentally. Luca would be angry with me if I killed him. At least right now. And if he'd seen us, he would've left me with no other choice. So I had to drug you to bring you here."

As panic rose within me, the rush of adrenaline in my blood removed some of the cobwebs from my mind and the sluggishness from my muscles. Not quite back to normal, but close. The room gradually came into focus as I braced my palms on the scratchy blanket beneath me and lifted my upper body, twisting around so I could see what kind of room I was in.

Not a room.

A cell.

Iron bars surrounded me on three sides, spaced about three inches apart. To my back was a wall. "What the hell?" I kept looking around me, convinced I was still dreaming. "Where the hell am I?"

"You're safe, Luna."

I knew that voice. My head snapped around. "Tristan?"

He stood to the right side of the cell door with his hands in his front pockets, just outside the bars, watching me with those emotionless dark eyes the way he always did.

"Tristen, why the fuck am I in a cell?"

"You weren't safe with Gino any longer. I was coming to get you out of there when I found you outside." He cocked his head. "Why were you outside? And why aren't you dressed?"

My head began to pound, and I put one hand on my forehead. "Because...because..." I tried to remember. Gino had come into my room, and he hadn't been himself. "Oh, my god. He had a gun."

Although he didn't move, his shoulders stiffened. "Who had a gun?" he asked quietly.

"Gino," I whispered. "He came to my room after you left. He was drunk, and he had a gun."

"What was he planning to do with it?"

Though the volume at which he spoke never changed, I could hear the anger in his voice. His entire body practically vibrated with it. I blinked against the light, but my eyes didn't want to focus. "I'm not sure," I lied. "I ran away." I didn't know why I didn't tell him the truth. Gino had come into my room to kill me. Or maybe he was going to kill both of us. I wasn't sure. But either way, I'd known the moment I saw him that I wasn't going to leave there alive.

The breath he released was audible. "So the blood on your skin and shirt doesn't belong to you?"

I looked down. The neckline of my tank top was streaked with dried blood. "No. It's Gino's. I bit him." I didn't tell him where. I could still taste the salty copper of his blood mixed with the metallic taste of the drugs. It made me want to puke.

"Good girl. But why didn't you use the knife I left you?"

"Yeah," I squinted up at him. "I didn't have a chance to grab it." I shivered. It was cold in the room, and I was still only wearing my sleep shorts and tank top. Looking around, I found the blanket I was sitting on and tried to tug it out from under my butt as I tried to keep the panic that continued to threaten under control. Freaking out wouldn't get me out of here. "It's so cold."

"Yes," he agreed, but he made no move to adjust the temperature.

"Tell me again why I'm here, Tristan." I knew he'd already told me, but I couldn't remember. Wrapping the blanket around my shoulders, I tried to get to my feet and fell back onto my butt.

"You're not safe at Gino's, so I brought you here, where I can protect you."

"You locked me in a cell to keep me safe?" I repeated, trying and failing to keep the disbelief from my voice. Oh god. Oh god. Oh god. I'd gone from being locked in a room to being locked in a fucking cell.

"Yes," he answered simply.

I tried to understand, but I was having a hard time keeping up with the conversation. My thoughts felt like they were swimming through sludge, even as adrenaline raced through my veins, urging me to run. It was a weird sensation. He watched me as I tried again to get to my feet, but offered no assistance. This time, I managed by using the wall behind me as leverage, my blanket falling from one shoulder. I shivered again as the air conditioner kicked on.

There was another door set into the wall behind me that I hadn't noticed at first. One that led into another room. Without thinking, I stumbled through it and into...a bathroom. It wasn't fancy, but it had everything a prisoner would need. A toilet. A sink. There was even a shower. No window, though. And no other doors.

"There are towels in the cabinet above the toilet along with the shampoo and body wash you like. There's also some extra toilet paper and tampons under the sink. They're the kind you use. If you need anything else, just let me know, and I'll get it for you."

I couldn't even respond at first as my drugged brain tried to comprehend what was happening. "I need you to let me out of here," I told him, one hand on the wall as I slowly made my way back out to the cell. "That's what I need." My legs felt like they weighed a thousand pounds.

He didn't respond.

I searched his eyes for any sliver of uncertainty or guilt about locking me in here. There was absolutely none. "Tristan. You need to let me out."

He shook his head. "No."

No? That's it? That's all he had?

"Tristan! You can't just lock me up like this!"

"It's the only place where you'll be safe, Luna."

"Safe from what?!" I screamed at him. Holy shit. This was so much more horrifying than being locked in my bedroom at Gino's. At least there I knew that if worse came to worse, I could just go out the window and run. But here, behind bars...

There was no escape from here.

"Tristan, you can't keep me in here. I have family. They'll be looking for me." My vision was slowly getting better. I looked around the room outside of the cell, searching for something, anything, that I could possibly use to help me escape. But the room was bare. All except for the gray walls, which were covered in pieces of white paper, all different sizes.

As I looked closer, I realized the paper wasn't plain. They were drawings. Mostly with pencil. A few with something darker. Maybe charcoal? And they were all images of...

Me.

Stunned, I stood in the middle of the cell with my feet braced and the blanket hanging off my one shoulder. My eyes went from one drawing to the next. There was one of me in the dress and fur I'd worn to the wedding, my hair tumbling around my shoulders and my eyes wide and slightly startled. Another of me lying in bed, my hair in a braid and headphones in my ears. Actually, there were a few of me in bed. Jesus, how many times had he snuck in and watched me sleep? There were some of me smiling, and some of me crying. There was even one of me pressed up against the window of my room, my skirt hiked up around my thighs, and a man's arm wrapped around my waist.

They were so realistic they were practically like photographs. "What is this?" I whispered.

He dug around in the inside pocket of his suit jacket and pulled out a cell phone. Tapping on the screen, he did something before squatting down and sliding it along the floor through the bars to me. "This is for you. So you can call your brother, and he doesn't worry about you."

I tore my eyes from the images on the walls and looked down at the phone. "He'll come looking for me. Someone will come looking for me." I didn't know if I was trying to convince him or myself.

"No," he told me. "He won't. Because if you say anything to him that leads him to believe you're anything but perfectly happy and just too busy to see him, I'll do whatever I have to do to keep him from leading Gino to you." There wasn't an ounce of emotion in his voice as he talked about killing my brother like he was nothing but a pesky fly. Because that was exactly what he was saying. I knew it all the way down to my bones.

Oh, my god. He was a fucking psycho. "You can't just keep me in here," I repeated.

He stared at me but said nothing. Desperately, I waited for him to tell me this was all some big fucking joke. But deep down in my bones, I knew it wasn't. He turned to leave, and I rushed toward him, grabbing at him through the bars as I screamed, "YOU CAN'T KEEP ME HERE!"

His eyes widened in alarm as he jumped back, just out of reach of my fingers, his chest rising and falling with fast, hard breaths.

I don't like to be touched.

We stared at each other. And in the silence, I heard his cell phone vibrate. Reaching into his inside jacket pocket, he pulled it out and tapped the screen with his thumb before tearing his eyes from mine. His eyebrows came together with a frown. Then he sighed heavily and slid his phone back into his jacket. "I'm sorry, but I have to leave for a while. You'll be safe here while I'm gone. I won't be long."

He kept saying I'd be safe. "Safe from who? Gino? Why do you keep telling me I'll be safe?" My voice was shrill, and I knew I sounded as crazy as I felt.

I thought, for a moment, he would answer me. But then he turned and walked toward the door that, I assumed, led out to the rest of the house. "I don't have time to get into it right now. I shouldn't be very long. The room is completely soundproof, so screaming will only be a waste of energy. When I return, I'll make you something to eat and we can talk more. The effects of the drugs will be worn off by then and you'll be feeling better." Leaving the room, he closed the door behind him. I heard the click of a lock.

"Tristan!" I screamed after him. "Tristan, please! Let me out of here!"

But there was nothing but complete silence.

I was all alone.

ABOUT THE AUTHOR

Hi! My name is Angel Rayne and I write dark, delicious romance with antiheroes who would burn down the world to save the woman they love. I never understood why the villains never win the girl, and so I decided to write them their own love stories where they do.

Here are a few other odds and ends about me...

-Music inspires my stories and I make playlists for every book.

-I am not a fast writer. My stories take time to write. They need to brew in my head. To have book releases close together I have to write ahead. But I would much rather take the time the stories need to be the best they can be than try to rush them out. Trust me on this one.

-I love the rain, and I'm happiest when I'm sitting in a coffee shop with my laptop as it storms outside.

-I prefer to go watch movies alone, with one of those fancy coffees hidden in my purse. (Yes, I really do this.)

-My husband calls me his "little bird" because anything that sparkles catches my eye.

-I will never have enough soft blankets. Ever.

-I love ALL THE DRAMA...but only in books.

-I will forever re-watch The Phantom of the Opera with the hope that by some miracle, this time Christine will choose the right guy.

Thank you for reading my stories, and I always love to hear from you! You can reach me at: angel@angelrayne.com